UNSTABLE FELICITY

*un*stable FELICITY

A Christmas Novella

Cat
HODGE

OAK &
LINDEN

For the big three, Eleanor, Julia, and Isabel, and young Diana, who are the best of sisters.
And for Jack, William, and Paul, because the boys are back in town.

... Tell me, my daughters,—
Since now we will divest us both of rule,
Interest of territory, cares of state,—
Which of you shall we say doth love us
    most?
That we our largest bounty may extend
Where nature doth with merit challenge.

— *KING LEAR,* ACT I, SCENE 1

O irreversible decrees of the Fates, that never swerve from your stated course! Why did you ever advance me to an unstable felicity ...?

— KING LEAR, QUOTED BY GEOFFREY OF
MONMOUTH, *HISTORY OF THE KINGS OF
BRITAIN*

CHAPTER 1

ON THE FIRST OF DECEMBER, JILL O'LEARY—UNTIL LAST week a self-possessed, self-assured career woman—found herself up in the air, obeying her mother's order to spend Christmas in Luxembourg.

"Luxembourg!" her coworker Amita Patel had squealed late Friday afternoon, as Jill shoved her laptop into her bag with hands that would not stop trembling. "I am so jealous! Forests, and mountains of snow, and probably a tall, dark, handsome prince looking for a normal American girl." She surveyed their unromantic office, home to one of Los Angeles's top accounting firms, and nestled glumly in her cardigan against the chill of the industrial HVAC. "And I'm stuck here in L.A. again, and not doing anything for Christmas, like the good little Hindu I am."

"Luxembourg, Ohio," said Jill, hoping her voice sounded wry and not bitter. "Where it rarely snows in December. We should trade places. I've spent the past twelve years avoiding family Christmas, like the bad little Catholic I am."

"Is Ohio your home?" Amita lit up. "Over Thanksgiving, I saw a Christmas movie set in a small town in Ohio, where the girl had to save her family's business by teaming up with the hot competitor, and he caught her when she fell off a ladder, and they got everyone to come together to fix up the old downtown. And then it snowed, and they lived happily ever after," she sighed, with a wistful glance from the 19th-story window down at the palm trees along Figueroa Street.

"That kind of feel-good fluff makes me hate the world," Jill snapped, zipping her bag with unnecessary force. "My home is here. I'm *from* Luxembourg. It's the kind of hick town you leave as soon as you're eighteen. If you're lucky."

Amita looked at her curiously. "If it upsets you so much, why go back?"

Suddenly Jill was sitting down, with her ears ringing and Amita gently slapping her cheeks. The tremors she had been fighting off ever since her phone rang now gripped all her muscles, or maybe it was just that she was trying so hard not to laugh. "Because my mother told me to. That's funny, isn't it?"

"Girl, I have an Indian mother," Amita murmured, kneading some life back into Jill's clammy hands. "You don't have to tell me."

"You think you're grown up." Jill could hear herself devolving into babble, but she couldn't stop herself. "You think after living on your own for twelve years, you can do what you want with your life. And then you find yourself sitting up and begging when Mother tells you to."

Amita eyed her with concern. "Are you all right?"

Jill had been through enough years of therapy to answer this question with confidence. "No, I am not all right. I was, until Mother called. I was so proud of myself for keeping it together since Daddy died. I thought I was grieving so sensibly. I wasn't sensible. I was just numb. And now I'm not numb anymore."

"Cut yourself some slack," Amita said gently. "Your dad only died four months ago."

"Only?" said Jill, not trying to hide the bitterness anymore. "That's not what my mother said today. She told me what an eternity it had been since I'd bothered to check on her. 'I could use your help, Gillian, if you could deign to come home for more than the two days it took to bury Daddy.' I felt sick just seeing her name on my phone. Even the sound of her voice made me want to throw something. Just like the good old days."

It was a testament to the persona Jill had built over the last twelve years that Amita should find this so incredible. "This is a side of you I've never seen."

This time Jill did laugh hysterically. "I don't want people to see this side of me."

"Not a happy home life, then?" Amita ventured.

"I loved my Dad a lot," said Jill, choking on the words. "But I made his life harder because I was always fighting with Mother." She stood up and smoothed her hair and clothes, trying to regain some semblance of her lost dignity. "I swore to myself after his funeral that I'd never go back again. And here I am, crawling home the first time Mother gives an order."

Amita picked up Jill's bag as well as her own. "But why do you have to go for all of December? Why not just fly in for Christmas and get out as soon as you can? No one would blame you."

"Mother would," said Jill darkly. "How fortunate for her

that she raised a Certified Public Accountant. Didn't I tell you? I'm going home to save the family business."

TWELVE YEARS. Twelve years since Jill O'Leary had last been home for Christmas, twelve years since she'd helped her family run the Luxembourg Inn, twelve years since she'd revved out of town in her rusting pickup truck, stopping only to run over Heath Albany's dog for good measure. At eighteen she'd thought there was no way she'd ever be going home again, so why not burn all her bridges at once? She'd considered actually setting fire to the covered bridge outside town, as a vengeful pun, but she hadn't wanted to make things harder for Daddy than they needed to be. He would have understood, though. "You take things so literally," he told her, as their private joke.

Now Daddy was dead, and Heath was married last she'd heard, and Jill was being summoned home for Christmas to save the Luxembourg Inn. "Summoned" had the dour ring of a court date, which wasn't a bad way to describe any occasion where Mother was likely to sit in judgment on your life and find it wanting. And Mother—perhaps Regina O'Leary's daughters had called her "Mama" before they'd learned to talk, but that was too casual a title for a woman who never unbent—had issued an ultimatum. "Gillian, if you don't find some way to fix the finances before Christmas, I will be forced to sell the Inn. I cannot carry this tax burden on my shoulders alone. Do you want to do that to your mother? Do you want to explain to your sisters why you wouldn't help save their inheritance?"

Jill doubted that her sisters would listen to any explanation from her, but all the same, she was going back to Luxembourg, Ohio, to rescue an inn she didn't care for, for a mother who'd never cared for her.

Jill couldn't detect the faintest whiff of nostalgia on touching down at the Columbus Airport, and she was unreasonably irked at having to rent a car. When Daddy was alive, there had always been six or seven cars sitting behind his garage that she could have used for free. Daddy was like that: buying cars on spec, fixing them up because he enjoyed doing it, and selling them at a loss to people who needed the help. There was probably also a tax write-off angle involved, because Daddy was like that, too. Of course, if Daddy were still alive she wouldn't have had to drive, because he would have picked her up. But Jill had not come home while Daddy was alive.

Heath Albany was running the garage now, she guessed. Daddy had always had a soft spot for Heath. As a teenager, Jill had found that infuriating. After all, she'd taken up with him to stick it to her parents, to prove her independence as destructively as possible. Mother had disapproved, of course.

"You can do better than that, Gillian," Regina O'Leary had said, adjusting her perfectly frosted hair with calculated dismissal. "It's tedious of you to act out this way, but if you want to bring home a brute, at least make sure he's housebroken."

Jill had expected Daddy to toss Heath out, or demand to know his intentions. Instead, Daddy had invited him to help at the garage. In the end Daddy and Heath were far more compatible than Jill and Heath had ever been. After all, Jill and Heath only had animal attraction between them. Daddy and Heath shared an interest in something outside themselves. Man to man, Heath was not ashamed to admit there were things he didn't know, and things he wasn't good at yet, which was more humility than he was willing to display in front of a girlfriend.

Jill hoped he'd gotten better at forgiving over the years, because they were probably going to have to talk about that dog.

HER HEART WAS NOT SOOTHED by the long drive past dull Ohio fields. Distant Luxembourg, her Ohio if any part of it was still hers, was not the flat golden heartland of Amita's Hallmark imagination. It was an isolated county of dense Appalachian forest. Only a mix of optimism and folly—or perhaps they were the same thing—could have incited desperate pioneers to carve settlements and hillside farms out of the heavy woods. The region had character, but it wasn't the glossy community pep of movies where all problems were solved in ninety minutes. It was a gritty, insular, suspicious ethic of survival bred by the encroaching forest, which might at any uncontested moment take back its own.

The woods were pressing around her now, opening here and there to allow for a small house or hard-won field. Not much had changed while she had been away. Development came to the big cities and the surrounding fields, where tracts of generic houses that would disintegrate in twenty years were devouring the rich land that used to feed America. Development came to the towns along the interstates, with wide lanes and gentle grades for semi trucks. Development did not come to places like hard-scrabble Luxembourg, fading towns on the way to somewhere else, far from the glory days of coal mining and rail junctions and opera houses and mountain spas.

And who in their right mind would build an inn in a place on no one's way, in a town no one wanted to visit? Her great-grandparents, that was who: entrepreneurs hoping to cash in on post-war tourism, architecturally savvy enough to commission a lodge now on the National Register of Historic Places as an early example of Mid-century Modern. Her mother never ceased reminding her that this was a family business, that people had obligations to family. You couldn't just walk away from an inn styled like a Swiss chalet, even though the actual Luxembourg was not in Switzerland, was in fact its own country that just wanted to be left alone. And when family called, even a successful accountant from Los Angeles left civilization and journeyed back into the primitive woods.

"Welcome to Luxembourg, population 5,000," boasted the sign at the town limits. Why 5,000? Jill wondered. Why anyone? Why does this town even exist? Here was old Main Street, the blocks of downtown wedged between the river and the forest, brick storefronts festooned with garlands and poinsettias. There was the sad covered bridge, long since bypassed by the Main Street bridge, which had been long since bypassed by Route 33. There, just beyond downtown, were the stone pillars and ornamental iron gates guarding the drive of the Luxembourg Inn. Halfway up the drive stood the white caretaker's house where Jill had grown up, front porch tastefully tricked out with Mother's holiday decor. And there, where the drive swept in an elegant circle around a fountain and a gazebo, was the hidden gem of the forest: the Luxembourg Inn itself, all half-timbering and balconies genteelly crumbling away under a quantity of evergreen swag.

As Jill pulled in to the gates, the first snowflakes began to fall. "Welcome home to Luxembourg," she thought, parking behind Mother's house. "Ho, ho, ho."

CHAPTER 2

"Just checking on you!" Amita's voice crackled as Jill fumbled with her phone in the middle of the night. "Did you make it in safely?

"Amita, it's one a.m.," Jill groaned, sitting up to get her bearings in the elegant guest room that no longer looked like her childhood bedroom.

"Oh, I forgot about the time difference!" Amita said, unrepentant. "Have you met any tall, dark, handsome strangers yet?"

"I have not. I got in late, said hello to Mother, and went straight to bed. And tomorrow morning, I'm setting straight to work, and I'll work until the job is done and I can get out of here. I don't have time for office romances."

"But surely there's at least one man in town who will discover that your big-city skills are just what he needs to save his farm," Amita insisted. "Find him. For my sake."

"My ex-boyfriend is still local," Jill admitted. "But last time I saw him, I killed his dog."

Amita was silent, pondering how to fix this relationship between commercial breaks. "Maybe it wasn't really dead. Maybe the dog miraculously recovered, and he's forgiven you. The boyfriend, I mean, not the dog."

"I ran over it with a pickup truck. Twice."

"Oh, Jill, that's bad."

"We were both bad," Jill said. "Anyway, I think he's married now."

"Maybe he's a widower with small children who need a mother's love?"

"*Amita.*"

"At least tell me that it's snowing," Amita pleaded. "You can't have come all this way for nothing."

Jill, pushing aside the lace curtains, could give her some glad tidings. "If it keeps coming down like this, we'll have a white Christmas."

JILL WAS ALMOST RECONCILED to the prospect of a white Christmas, if only for the sake of Amita's Midwestern ideal, but she had no intention of being dragooned into Mother's White Elephant party.

"But darling," said Mother, coming into the downstairs office yet again, where Jill had been secluded with the hotel accounts for the past few days, "I always have a White Elephant party on the first Saturday of December, in the lobby of the Inn. Everyone is so excited to see you again. Your sisters will be there. Even hotel guests can come, if they wish."

Years of therapy had finally persuaded Jill not to indulge her first impulse to snap back if she wasn't committed to a fight. Instead of suggesting that Mother try nagging the guests all week and see if they still wished to come, she simply said, "I didn't bring a present."

"Oh, it doesn't have to be anything expensive. Just take something you find sitting around."

"Sounds like stealing."

"No one brings anything valuable to a White Elephant exchange," Mother said, sidestepping the ethical question. "That would defeat the purpose. You bring something that has no value to you, and you trade for something that has no value to someone else. It's environmentally friendly. Reagan is bringing a pair of holiday Crocs."

"Crocs aren't cheap."

"Yes, but nobody values them."

Jill sat back from the table covered with tax returns and receipts and various papers she'd been trying to sort, and let out her breath in a controlled fashion that could not be called a sigh.

"I'd hoped to relax tonight, Mother. All finances and no play make Jill a dull girl."

"I know, darling. I've barely seen you since you came home. After twelve years you might at least eat dinner with me. I know you only had two days to attend your father's funeral, but now that you can spare some time, I think we ought to see more of each other."

What Jill was seeing was red, clouding her vision, taking her back to the days when Mother could and did get under her skin, until shouting and smashing seemed the only way out. I'm not eighteen anymore, she thought. I'm an adult. I will not be provoked. Find a compromise.

"I suppose you'll see me this evening at your White Elephant party, if it's that important to you," she said, with mostly unforced graciousness. "Until then, my first priority is the job that you called me home to do."

"Well, I can't wait to see what you've come up with," Mother declared. "Your father poured his heart into his businesses to support this family. I know you won't let that Garrett French get away with another lowball offer for the Inn. You were always Daddy's girl. Don't undervalue his work."

And Mother shut the door gently, leaving Jill to choke on her responses. I don't "come up" with numbers! The figures are all here. They exist. They are solid, indisputable, comfortingly discoverable facts. The inn is worth what it's worth, no matter how much you or I or Daddy valued it.

"That Garrett French" was the stock villain of Mother's life, an investor who now owned half of downtown. According to which mood Mother was in, he was either impeding progress by refusing to modernize outdated buildings, or destroying history by recklessly renovating the crumbling charm out of the historic district. Jill imagined him as Old Man Potter, rubbing his hands and cackling as he lowballed the worthy property owners of Luxembourg, Ohio.

Jill stretched and then shivered in the chill of the old house. She was at work in Daddy's old office, where she'd been practically imprisoned ever since she arrived, with orders to spin straw into gold. No, that was being unfair. She knew, if she cared to cast her mind back, that Mother had an array of snacks out for her in the kitchen as she'd lugged her bags into the house, and that she'd slept late each morning in her renovated bedroom. The bedroom, just like the office and the rest of the house, was spotless and fresh. Jill suspected, though she could not get a clear answer out of Mother, that the Inn staff were cleaning this house along with their standard housekeeping duties next door. And the books were being fudged so that somehow this counted as a business expense. So many things, in fact, counted as business expenses that the Inn was barely running at a profit. And the same went for Daddy's garage, and several other ventures that fell under the heading of "family business."

The implications of this needed to be hashed out, but for now, all Jill wanted was something warm to wear. She pulled open the closet door in the front hall before she remembered that she didn't live here anymore and wouldn't have a jacket hanging up. And then, as she stared at Daddy's old Christmas sweater sagging on its wooden hanger, she felt her heart contracting into a leaden lump of grief.

It was in the closet because he'd worn it all year round, and because in the four months since his death no one had had the heart to move it. Here it was in all its mothballed, faded, oversized glory. Oversized for Daddy, anyway; he'd never been a big man. Red, with holly leaves, and in the center a big white "Ho^3." That was Daddy's kind of humor. He'd seen fit to wear it on balmy spring days as well as by the glow of the Yule log. Jill pulled the sweater on and wrapped herself in her father. Here she was in his arms again, pressing her face against his shoulder, smelling his warm Daddy smell, wiping her tears on this very sleeve. Why had she not come home? Why had she let her mother keep her away? Why did she think emails and calls could substitute for Daddy in his sweater?

The big sob she could no longer hold in broke forth,

and with it all the temper that she'd so carefully curbed for the past week, and the past twelve years. A string of chaste white lights, framing the front door, was within her grasp. She jerked them down with a familiar burst of childish satisfaction and yanked the door open to hurl them out onto the porch. And with a horrified jolt back into adulthood, she stayed her arm just in time to avoid hitting the hat of the man just outside the door, stamping the snow off his shoes.

Finally, Amita's made-for-TV fantasies were coming true, in a fashion. Here was the classic tall, dark, handsome stranger on her doorstep. Tall: not much more so than Jill herself, but with a lean and hungry look. Dark: not much more so than the standard ruddy peasantry of Luxembourg County, but a Black man, nonetheless. Handsome, oh yes: no callow youth, but a man with the fathomless brown eyes of one who has endured and must keep on enduring. His shoes and his long coat were several cuts above Luxembourg standards of formality. And, most delightful, he was wearing a hat, a fedora or a homburg or whatever it was that men of the world wore in old movies.

His flinch at her upraised arm brought Jill to her senses, and she realized how she must look to him. He was not getting an eyeful of Hollywood polish, but of crazed elf: ancient Christmas sweater, frizzy black hair, red eyes and blotchy face, nose welling up with a big drip, and the bulbs of fury still glowing in her fist. She hadn't even pulled them out of the plug.

"Trouble with your lights?" asked the man, who had recovered himself as well. "Can I do anything to help?"

Jill had already formulated a story about the difficulties

of Christmas decorating when her mouth said instead, "I was angry."

He took in the Christmas sweater, and asked, "Are you Gillian?"

"Jill, yes," she said, too startled to deny her full name. "How did you know?"

"Well, you're holding lights, and you'll forgive me if I note that you are not dressed to the uniform standard of the Luxembourg Inn staff members that Regina pulls in to do her menial household tasks."

Jill started ugly-laughing. "I'm sorry," she choked, "but you don't know how refreshing it is to hear someone come out and say that she uses Inn employees to do her housework. Does she pay them under the table, or is she cooking the books?"

"Probably the latter," the man said, and he seemed to understand why the question mattered. "I used to see your dad wearing that sweater all the time. Now here is someone else in Chuck O'Leary's Christmas sweater—out of love, I assume, because no one would wear it otherwise. You look like your sisters Reagan and Del, but I can't imagine either of them wearing your dad's sweater or crying. So, a family member: the prodigal daughter coming home to paper over the accounting problems. Which would make anyone understandably angry. Ergo, Gillian. Or Jill, if you prefer."

"Love" was a word that Jill had heard her mother say often over the years, in many different contexts. She thought it was a word that could no longer have any effect on her. But now, to hear someone cite the Christmas sweater as evidence that she genuinely loved her father destroyed her for a moment.

The man waited patiently while she tried to pull herself back together.

"Are you okay?" he asked, offering her a tissue. "Is there anything I can do?"

Jill hiccuped through her sobs. "Did you really just say 'ergo'?"

He laughed. "I did. I'm pompous that way."

The sweater was as convenient as the soggy tissue, so she wiped her eyes and nose on it as well. "I'm sorry," she snuffled, and then she was angry again. "Though there's no reason I should apologize. I can cry if I want to."

"You don't have to apologize for that at all," he said. "Your dad was a good man."

Jill wailed. "And I didn't even hit you with the lights, so I don't have to be sorry for that either. Why were you standing right outside the door?"

"I won't be, much longer. I can see this isn't a good time."

"Is it that obvious?"

He smiled, but without mockery. Something about his face, a bit too worn, a bit too thin, hinted that he'd hit a low point himself once. Trying to wrest back some shreds of her lost social competence, Jill said, "I assume you're here to see my mother. Would you like to come in and wait for her?"

He hesitated, but Jill thought she saw a startled spark of life behind his reserve. Boldly, she upped the ante. "I can offer you a drink."

He took a step back. With a shock, she recognized the same snapping down of restraint that she herself had cultivated to deal with Mother.

"Thanks, but could you please tell Regina that I'll stop by to see her another time?"

He handed Jill a business card and tipped his old-school hat to her as he turned to go. What was that all about? Jill wondered, watching him walk off in his long wool coat. Who wears a hat? Who says ergo?

Looking down at the card, she read the name "Garrett French."

CHAPTER 3

SATURDAY AFTERNOON FOUND JILL NOT ACCOUNTING, not relaxing, not hunting for just the right gift for the White Elephant party, but shivering on the sidewalk along Main Street in the company of her two sisters, watching the Hometown Christmas parade pass by. Main Street glowed: reproduction gas lamps flickered, shop windows beckoned, and sunbeams diffused through the snowflakes to create the sourceless illumination of a Thomas Kinkade painting. From a passing car the scene would have been entirely charming. Standing out in it, Jill was miserably aware that she had acclimated to the seasonless warmth of Los Angeles. Her cropped coat didn't keep out the chill. Her toes were numb. The only thing that warmed her was the sight of snowflakes hitting the paraders right in the face as they marched.

Reagan and Del were impervious to the cold in their individual get-ups. Del, the youngest of the three sisters, was wrapped in a Doctor Who scarf (Tom Baker, of course) and a Lands' End parka she'd bought the year

Captain America was in theaters. Reagan, Jill's older sister, sported a North Face parka and matching cashmere gloves and scarf. Her hat sat lightly on her blond locks (bleached; the O'Learys were Black Irish). Under her gloves, her manicure was unchipped. Wedge boots lined with fur raised her almost to Jill's height. Her manner was as honeyed as her hair, and just as studied.

"I pulled a few strings to get the dance studio's float second to last in the parade, right before Santa," she bragged, with the little laugh that had always set Jill's teeth on edge. "Quennedey's going to be Clara. Her class were all supposed to be mice, but I told Miss Gabi I wouldn't put the deposit on the float if she was going to put Quennedey in an ugly fur suit."

Jill had never met young Quennedey, but the photos she had seen of Reagan's daughter did not suggest that she would make a very winsome Clara. Perhaps the snow would soften her glower.

What Jill only thought, Del came right out and said. "Why do you make that kid take ballet? She hates it. If you're trying to relive your youth, get plastic surgery. At least then only you have to suffer."

"Isn't our Del charming?" drawled Reagan in an accent that Jill classified as "catalog country." "Baby of the family, always gets to say whatever she wants. Del has every word in her vocabulary but 'tact.'"

"At least I'm still married," said Del, which shut Reagan up.

Back in the middle, thought Jill. Reagan all sugar and Del all spice. And me, I'm not even in the same cupboard. I'm more like the liquor cabinet. Maybe I'm the bourbon

—kinda rough going down, but warm inside? Does that even mean anything?

Shaking off her metaphors, she asked, "Are we supposed to bring gag gifts to the White Elephant party tonight? How expensive are we talking? Who's coming, anyway?"

"You want to play it safe," Reagan advised. "Everyone's going to be there, even hotel guests. Get something classy that you could give to anyone."

"Just pull something out of a closet," said Del. "That's what I'm going to do. The cheaper and tackier, the better."

A float for Vineyard Fellowship moved toward them, blaring "Mary, Did You Know?" Mary and Joseph were a pair of teenagers staring adoringly at a doll in a manger. The shepherds, in cowboy hats, kept watch over a herd of fluffy sheep. Wise men pitched candy out to children, who darted into the street and squabbled over Tootsie Rolls and Starbursts.

Del was irate. "I called every single registered group in the parade and told them that this year we should ban candy tossing. It leaves litter all along the parade route, and it's irresponsible. Some child could get hit running out in the road."

"Has that ever happened?" Jill asked.

"No, and I'd like to keep it that way."

Jill wanted to argue the point, but as the Vineyard float pulled even with them, she recognized the cowboy at the wheel: Heath Albany, a little older, a little heavier, a wedding ring definitely on his hand. He nodded at Reagan, then Del, and then his eyes met Jill's. The float ground to a halt. Jill's pulse pounded as she measured her effect on him after all these years. Then she realized that Heath had stopped because the cop at the corner had paused the parade to let the backed-up traffic through the intersection.

"Jill!" Heath called to her. There was a thrilling nervousness in his voice she'd never heard when they were younger. She stepped out into the street without exactly willing it. Maybe it was good that their first meeting would be in full view of the public. They'd never been good for anything in private but fighting or ... Jill felt the snowflakes melting on her hot cheeks.

"Heath," she said, reaching for a generic, unfraught greeting. "How's business?"

"Good, good," he said, taking her literally. "The shop is doing great. This is one of our trucks, actually. Everything's going well."

"That's ... nice."

"I'm running the place just as your dad would have wanted me to," he said, and the flash of his smile pulled Jill back to the days when Heath and Daddy worked side by side, man to man. "Maybe you'd like to come around to the garage sometime, for old times' sake."

It was an innocent enough suggestion, but the hesitant intensity behind the invitation put Jill deliciously on her guard.

"I heard you got married," she said significantly. To her surprise, his face brightened with a pride that seemed out of keeping from a man who'd pretty much just propositioned her.

"Yeah, that's my son," he said, motioning back at one of the children on the float, a tiny bored sheep absorbed in an iPad.

Jill felt expected to say something, so she asked, "How old?"

"He's five now," said Heath. "Jill, listen, I have to talk to you. You're the only one who ..."

The parade lurched into motion once again.

"I'll be at the shop," called Heath. Jill stood in the street and watched him looking back at her in his mirror as the float moved on. And then Del pulled her onto the sidewalk, out of the path of the high school marching band.

"Are you going to get your claws back into Heath Albany?" asked Reagan, with apparently genuine interest.

"My taste doesn't run to married men," said Jill with dignity. "I'm sure he just wants to catch up."

"A man like that only has one thing on his mind," Del said.

"You think so?" said Jill, not sure whether to be flattered or affronted. "He did introduce me to his son."

"I don't mean sex," Del said. "I mean his mind isn't big enough to hold more than one idea at a time. See you later." She strode off down the street, having reached her quota of sister time for one afternoon.

"Quennedey!" Reagan bellowed. Jill turned to see a majestic Christmas tree drifting past, surrounded by toy soldiers and mice and snowflakes with brightly rouged cheeks and perfect ballet buns. Clara and her prince sat on thrones, graciously greeting their subjects. Clara's gelled golden ringlets and lipstick smile remained serene as Reagan bawled at her.

That looks like a child who almost deserves the name Quennedey-with-a-Q, Jill thought. Then she saw that Reagan was not glaring at the oblivious Clara, but at a girl sitting next to the driver, wearing a black beret jammed down to her bushy eyebrows. As she saw her mother, she flicked her hand in a wave that somehow seemed to involve mainly her middle finger.

"I'll kill her," Reagan hissed. "Does she know how much I had to shell out for that truck to guarantee she'd be Clara?"

The tilt of Quennedey's beret suggested that she was reveling in her mother's every wasted dollar. Jill resolved to treat her niece to hot chocolate at the earliest opportunity.

As the parade wound to a close, the sisters strolled down Main Street. Jill browsed the windows of the various shops, looking for an elegant yet tacky gift in an acceptable price range. Suddenly Reagan seized her elbow, drawing her up short.

"It's him," she whispered. Jill craned her neck, searching for Heath Albany or maybe Garrett French, but Reagan was dragging her toward a tall, dark, handsome stranger.

"Mr. Singh," she purred. "So good to see you. Have you met my sister Jill? She's back in town for Christmas. Jill, this is Amit Singh, one of our guests at the Luxembourg Inn."

Jill was staring, and she knew it, but Mr. Singh had to be accustomed to this reaction from women. He had the almost inhuman beauty of the demigods of old, burdened neither with the awkwardness of youth nor the cares of age. And he clearly had a demigod's allowance, if his tailoring was any evidence.

To her astonishment, Mr. Singh bowed to her. "I have been enjoying your mother's hospitality at the

Luxembourg Inn," he said, his voice as warm as smoked curry.

"Will you be staying with us long?" Jill asked, taking refuge in the standard phrase of front-desk hospitality. This polished man seemed as if he'd be more at home in *Luxembourg* Luxembourg than the Ohio version.

"For a few weeks," he said. "I find this region entirely charming."

"Is that so?" What Jill had intended as a polite nothing came out as an incredulous snort. She attempted to salvage her manners. "Maybe it takes a fresh set of eyes."

"You see no potential in your hometown?" Mr. Singh shook his head with urbane regret.

"We've just been looking for presents for the White Elephant party tonight," Reagan cooed. "Mr. Singh will be joining us, Jill. He's dying to see what a small-town Christmas celebration looks like."

Jill's eyeroll must have been too obvious, for Mr. Singh smiled and said, "The Christmas spirit does not appeal to everyone."

To her horror, Jill automatically replied, "I wish I had some Christmas spirits."

"Can't wait to see you tonight!" said Reagan hastily, nudging Jill along.

Mr. Singh held out his hand to Jill. As she took it, he moved a step closer to her. She breathed in the distant perfume of the maharajahs as he murmured in her ear, "May I recommend Kumar Brothers Liquor on Route 33?"

KUMAR BROTHERS WAS INDEED worthy of Mr. Singh's recommendation. When Jill dropped his name, the younger Mr. Kumar nodded sagely and led her to one of the few obtainable bottles of Eagle Rare bourbon in the nation. The purchase made, the liquor was nestled into a padded box and wrapped in a heavy paisley paper that smelt faintly of cardamom. It would stand out among the pile of White Elephant gifts, which was convenient since Jill meant to end up with it herself.

Who on earth was Mr. Singh? she wondered. What brought him to the Luxembourg Inn? Why did Mr. Kumar breathe his name with reverence? How could anyone be so regally handsome and yet have such deferential grace? It was almost as if he were ...

"A prince!" sighed Jill. For one blissful moment she forgot that she was thirty years old and had outgrown fairy tales. She envisioned Mr. Singh in a cape and turban, riding in state on an elephant, acknowledging his subjects with a sedate wave. Come to that, maybe she had seen him like that, in one of Amita's Bollywood movies. What if he were an actor, scouting out locations for his next film! Did actors scout locations themselves? What kind of Bollywood movie could you shoot in the wilds of Ohio?

These satisfying reveries occupied her for most of the way back to town, a different route than she'd yet driven on this trip. Carefully rounding a sharp curve at the edge of her family's property so as not to skid in the snow, she passed a huge silver maple tree just outside the gates of the Inn. As far back as she could remember, this tree had always been there, a comforting sign that she was nearly home. In those days, it stood straight as a sentinel by the gates. Now it was unfamiliar and wrong, listing away from her at an alien angle. As her headlights flashed across the branches, a raccoon glared at her and dove into a hollow high in the trunk. Jill shivered and pulled up the driveway. The bottle of Eagle Rare seemed more appealing than ever, somehow.

Del was leaving the house as Jill came in.

"I'm all set for tonight," she said. "Here it is, cheap as it comes. I even wrapped it in Mother's newspaper." She held out a box covered in the weekend section of the Wall Street Journal.

"I don't think Mother had read that yet," said Jill.

"She can read it if she picks this box," said Del, heading toward the Inn.

Jill inventoried the slim pickings in her suitcase. Everyone was going to be at the party, Reagan had said. The mysterious Mr. Singh would be there. Heath, blue-collared and rough of hand. And Garrett French, with his hat and his "ergo." What did one wear to leave a lasting impression on three very different men? It was an academic question, as there was only one option in this case: a little black dress.

She surveyed herself in the hall mirror as she pulled on her coat. Black dress, plaid scarf, red lipstick—so simple, so forgettable. And above her head, the dull gleam of white berries. She looked up to find a ball of mistletoe hanging from the ceiling. Dragging Mother's heavy antique side table into the middle of the floor, she scrambled up, broke off a sprig, and tucked it in her bun. Whatever happened tonight, she would be prepared.

CHAPTER 4

JILL'S IMAGE OF THE LUXEMBOURG INN, FILTERED
through burnished childhood memories, was of a perfectly
mod time capsule: every brass ash tray gleaming, every
divan perfectly tufted, every hanging pendant with its
wooden accent. As *Mad Men* chic brought the mid-century
aesthetic back in vogue, she had begun to think of the Inn
as vintage rather than passé. And now, stepping out of
Mother's house into the wintery twilight, she allowed
herself, for the first time since her arrival, to drop her
jaded adult armor. Everyone was arriving, and the Inn
shone forth with the full glory of a Camelot-era Christmas.

Clutching her gift, she allowed herself to be swept
through the Inn's double doors with the press of arriving
guests. In the center of the lobby she turned, coat
swinging around her, ready to relive the magical Christmas
parties of her childhood. Everything was there: the lights,
the spice, the noble tree glowing against the backdrop of
the picture window. She had finally come home.

But she'd let her armor slip too soon. Like the slanted

silver maple by its gates, the entire hotel was off kilter. The tension between her memories and the reality before her paralyzed her like a slap. The lobby had shrunk somehow, until its grand reception area was no more than an oversized living room. The rich pile of the carpet was faded and flat. The woodwork, the pendants, the brass — everything had grown old, but it had not grown beautiful. What should have been improved was not even being maintained. In a distant, analytical, adult part of her mind, Jill was doing terrible calculations about how much cash would need to be infused into the Inn to make it live again. The answer confirmed that the Inn was going to die, and very soon.

"Darling!" her mother called, bearing down on her. "I wondered what could be taking you so long when we have guests."

Guests she had indeed, for she tugged Garrett French along like a trout on a line. Garrett was too polite to physically resist her, but he refused to let her hustle him.

"Now I want you to meet Garrett French," said Mother, squeezing his arm as if she were fond of him. "Such a dear boy."

Garrett's narrowed brown eyes met Jill's startled ones. The phrasing had just enough ambiguity that Jill couldn't tell whether Mother was playing dominance games with Garrett on social or racial grounds, but either way it was unacceptable.

"Mr. French and I met earlier today," Jill said, with full emphasis on the honorific. "I'm looking forward to doing business with him."

"You have to help me set him straight," Mother continued, paying her no heed. "I want you to tell him just how much this place is worth. Not just the worth in dollars. The value, the investment in time, in community, in family." She surveyed her tinsel-draped fiefdom with satisfaction. "Look around. Have you ever seen the Inn as magnificent as it is tonight?"

She believes, thought Jill, with a sinking heart. For Mother, the glamor of the Inn was as real now as it was when Jill was a child.

"Of course, the Inn holds a special place in all our hearts," said Garrett, detaching himself from Mother's grasp. Jill could see him doing what she had so often been unable to do: tailoring his words to Regina, speaking her language so that she would hear him. "It deserves to remain magnificent for years to come. But worth is not the same thing as value. If you don't act soon, value is all the Inn will have left."

"Well, I can understand how it would be hard for you of all people to value a parent's legacy," said Regina, smiling beautifully. "You speak to the man of money, Jill. Don't undervalue your inheritance. You, at least, loved your father."

"Love," whispered Jill, to Mother's back disappearing amid the guests. "I love him still."

"What a gift it must be," Garrett remarked, "to know exactly how to wound." He laughed, but his hands hung wooden by his side. "Nothing is abstract with Regina. Every disagreement must be personal."

"I don't think she does it only to be cruel." Some novel and disagreeable impulse of family loyalty drove Jill to defend her mother. "She's never really known herself. She thinks she's winning if she can make you change, and she'll say what comes into her mind whether it's fair or not. Del does it too, only Del always tells the truth and she doesn't care if you change."

"What happens when Mother finally gets her change?" said Garrett, with only a hint of acidity. "Does the other person ever get to speak his mind? Or does this dynamic only hold as long as someone else is willing to be the adult in the room?"

"Look, you're talking about my mom," said Jill, boiling into defensive anger against the raw familiarity of these questions. "She's a bitch, and she's always been a bitch. You'll have to change your expectations, because there's no point in trying to change her. You can't even dent her. Only God could get through to her, and you're not God."

She armed herself to unseat him in the next joust. But he did not spar with her. The terrible weight of his stillness against the din of the party was more disarming than any witty jab.

"No," he said at last. "I'm certainly no one's higher power."

Then the swirl of the crowd pushed them apart. Garrett made no effort to rejoin her. I've just made an enemy, Jill thought, and the feeling that welled up in her, stripped of its earlier rage, was strangely like grief.

She wanted to find her sisters. She wanted to eat. She wanted to slip into a dark room with Heath and see if the old passion could dull the old pain. What she did not want was to be part of a large, laughing group, and yet the White Elephant exchange was already being convened. Her gift was taken from her and added to a large pile, and the game began.

. . .

THE WHITE ELEPHANT party had become a tradition after Jill's time. The rules seemed clear to everyone but her. She saw Reagan instructing Mr. Singh in the finer points of retaining your chosen gift against all challenges. Mr. Singh caught Jill's eye across the room and smiled in the gentle way of the man who need fight for no gift because he already has everything. Quennedey inspected the gifts and shook one or two of the more intriguing packages. Del sat large and serene, her husband nestled in her shadow. Garrett French was exactly opposite Jill, across the mound of packages.

And Heath Albany appeared beside her. In his good suit, he looked almost as chiseled as he'd been twelve years ago. He was bearing two drinks, and he handed one of them to Jill.

"You look like you need this," he said.

"God, I do."

While Mother gave a welcoming speech and reminded everyone of the White Elephant procedure, Heath whispered, "You look amazing."

"Do I?" said Jill. "Glad I haven't let myself go after all these years."

"Your dad missed you. He was always telling me your news, about your jobs and your vacations. Sounds like you're doing well." He swallowed his drink. "Getting out of town was good for you."

"That's not exactly how you felt about my leaving, the last time we talked."

"I was wrong about a lot of things."

He was looking directly at her. She could sense the effort it took to say those words, and to meet her eyes as he said them. Instead of seeing the boy he'd been under the heavier features of the man, she could see the man he was now as a maturation of the boy. Perhaps she and the man would be more compatible than she and the boy.

He raised his glass and said, "To better times."

"To better times."

Mother finished with her opening remarks, and the White Elephant began. Jill, having missed the whole explanation of how to play the game, almost rose to grab her paisley-wrapped box, but realized that people were taking turns around the circle, and she was somewhere in the middle. Del started off the play by selecting an oversized bag and pulling out a pink camo snuggie, to cheers from the room. And then almost immediately, someone took it away from her. Apparently, you could pick an unopened present or trade for a gift someone else had already opened. Jill began to keep a watch on her box. That bourbon was going home with her, by hook or by crook.

There was a lot of hook and crook going on. The pink camo snuggie was hotly contested, but Del fixed her eye on it with determination. It wasn't the gift she'd brought; the newsprint box was still in the pile. Jill selected her own paisley present and opened her bourbon. She was prepared to fight all comers, but no one challenged her.

Next to her, Heath opened an Otterbox phone case. "Come on, Mom!" Quennedey said loudly enough to be heard over the room. "Are you going to trade for it?"

"Of course not," said Reagan. "Why would I want that phone case?"

"*I* want that phone case," said Quennedey.

Reagan opened a holiday scarf that was acceptable to her. Mr. Singh was enchanted to discover Big Mouth Billy Bass, the singing fish. To great applause, Garrett French found a Jackalope, a gag that made an appearance year after year. One of the last guests picked up Del's box and tore off the newsprint. Peeking inside, he whooped and held up a terrible Christmas sweater, red with holly leaves, featuring a big white "Ho^3."

Heath cheered as well. "The dad sweater! Awesome. I haven't seen it for ages." He turned to nudge Jill, but she'd risen from her seat.

"How could you do that, Del? Dad's sweater!" hissed Jill in her sister's ear.

"It was just sitting in the closet," said Del. "No one wanted it. I thought it would be funny." It was like Del to finally develop a sense of humor just in time to toss out a family heirloom.

Jill sat down again, the ringing in her ears mercifully drowning out the howls from the sweater brigade. Why had she not packed away Dad's sweater today? How could she have hung it back up so casually after crying in it? She clutched the newly worthless bourbon. Perhaps she could strike a private bargain now that the game was over, and get her sweater back.

But the game wasn't over. In the second round, people were passing or trading again, and the mood was getting intense. Jill readied herself for the main chance. As soon as her turn came, she pushed her bourbon at the jovial fellow and seized her sweater from his lap. The trading passed on. Jill folded the sweater carefully and made ready to pack it up. And as soon as she'd gotten it neatly arranged, someone took it from her and gave her Reagan's holiday Crocs. She stared at them, too stunned to follow the next several turns. The game was over, and she'd lost a piece of Dad.

"We're not done yet," said Quennedey, popping up behind Jill's chair. "There's one last round. I'm going to make my mom get the phone case, and then I'm going to lick it so no one else wants to touch it."

In the lull between rounds, Jill dragged her chair over by Del. Maybe it wasn't quite according to Hoyle to switch places during the game, but she needed to get her hands on the sweater as soon as possible.

The round started. Del, having acquired the pink camo snuggie, refused to trade, and her husband was content with his Christmas socks. Jill bounded up, declared for the sweater, and sat back in relief after ridding herself of the Crocs. Maybe she could sneak out of the game and get the sweater stowed safely in her suitcase.

But possession was not nine-tenths of the law in a White Elephant exchange. While Jill was still contemplating her plan, a lady wearing a reindeer antler headband swooped down and snatched the sweater out of her hands. "Gotta have this!" she crowed, leaving Jill with a box of chocolates and the urge to strangle her. Jill turned to Heath to beg him to trade for it, but he'd already lifted the Jackalope from Garrett French. She stared hard at Reagan, but Reagan's loyalties lay with Quennedey and her Otterbox. Mr. Singh did not part with his singing bass. Jill's chocolates were taken away, and her own bourbon returned to her.

And then Garrett French stood up with his gift, a curious, probably priceless brass objet d'art contributed by Mr. Singh, and traded it for Daddy's sweater. He returned to his seat amid much laughter, and folded the sweater on his lap without looking at Jill. She could not read his expression. How could he sit there so coolly, knowing as he did how much it meant to her? Had she offended him so much this evening that he needed to make this petty gesture of triumph over her, over the whole condescending O'Leary family? Was it some twisted form of kindness, his little way of letting her know that her dad's sweater would have a good home now?

She could be still no longer. The game wasn't over yet, but some fool might yet steal the sweater away. She was on her feet, almost stumbling across the room, thrusting the bottle of bourbon at him.

"Trade you," she said.

A murmur rippled through the room like the after-shock of a quake. In the hush that followed, Del irrelevantly hummed a snatch of "O Christmas Tree." Garrett sat with the same blank courtesy he'd displayed the other day on Mother's porch. He took the bourbon and set it deliberately on the floor, then surrendered the sweater. Jill retreated to a corner of the room and hugged it to herself, but no one else looked at her prize, or at her. In fact, the entire game seemed to drift apart. She had put her foot in it somehow, ruined everyone's fun, but no matter. Dad's sweater was hers, by right of affection and of conquest. She let the intensity of this conviction drown out any shame about her methods. Garrett knew what this meant to her. If he had a shred of humanity, he would understand and forgive.

Reagan edged up to her. "That was charming," she said, with a strange new respect in her voice. "I didn't know you had it in you, Jill. I always knew you could explode, but calculated humiliation is new for you."

"What do you mean?"

"Making him take that alcohol in front of everyone, I

mean. Didn't you know Garrett French is a drunk? Twelve Steps and everything. And how could he refuse you when you made such a deal of it? You must have wanted that old thing badly enough."

The righteous intoxication drained out of her, leaving only a sickening sobriety. "I did," said Jill faintly. "I thought I did."

Mother, who as hostess had not participated in the gift exchange, now joined them. "Darling," she gushed. "What a display! You certainly took Garrett French down a peg or two. I'm so proud to see you standing up for Daddy like that."

"Daddy wouldn't have been proud of me," protested Jill in an agony of self-immolation. "Daddy didn't humiliate anyone."

"Who said anything about humiliation?" said Mother. "Garrett shouldn't come to parties if he can't handle even the idea of alcohol. It's an obvious present at a White Elephant."

Jill broke free. Garrett was nowhere to be seen. Why would he want to hang around? To talk to her? To be publicly insulted again? She pulled on her coat and started for the door.

Mr. Singh appeared at her side and held it open for her. "Good evening, Miss O'Leary." He raised her hand to his lips. "I pay my respects to your mistletoe."

Jill stared at him blankly before she remembered. Patting her hair, she found the sprig and pulled it from her bun. As she contemplated her wreck of an evening, Del passed by and plucked the mistletoe from Jill's hand. "You won't be needing that," she said, and she held it over her husband's head and gave him a loud kiss.

.   .   .

OUTSIDE, the snow was falling more thickly than ever. The frosty peace of the evening was broken by the sound of tires whining and slipping in the parking lot as the first guests departed. In the gazebo in the lawn, away from the noise, a cigarette glowed red. Garrett French stood there in his hat and long coat, looking out toward the distant silver maple. Jill crossed the dark lawn and stood awkwardly at the entrance of the gazebo, twisting the sweater in her hands.

"Can I give this back to you?" said Garrett, holding out the bottle of bourbon to her without turning to face her.

"Thanks," said Jill, though that didn't seem the right thing to say. The cold neck of the bottle numbed her fingers. After a moment she offered, "Do you want the sweater back?"

"No, thanks," said Garrett. "I only took it so I could give it to you."

"Oh," said Jill, small and humbled, and thrilled. Silence stretched between them as a surge of people poured out of the Inn heading for the parking lot. Loudest among them was Heath Albany, crooning with boozy confidence about the state of his heart last Christmas.

"The blasted Heath," murmured Garrett.

Jill felt that this public display of drunkenness laid an obligation on her to open the subject. "Look, I'm very sorry. I had no idea. I thought you took the sweater to spite me."

"Why would I do that?"

"Because I was offensive earlier."

"*You* were offensive?" He seemed to think this amusing. "How?"

"Because I said you weren't God."

Garrett laughed, a sound free of rancor. "I'm not."

"Neither am I," said Jill, suddenly shaking. "I treated you terribly tonight, but please believe that it was only honest self-absorbed desperation, not ..." She tried to remember his phrasing from earlier this evening. "... Not an attempt to wound you. I'm not my mother. I've been gone for years. How could anyone expect me to know I shouldn't shove a bottle at you?"

"Are you asking me whether you should have been expected to know I was alcoholic, or telling me that everyone expects you to be rude?"

Jill swallowed. "That's fair. People here probably do expect me to be rude. It's what I used to be known for. Sometimes it's harder to change people's perceptions of you than to change yourself." She looked at the bourbon in her hands and writhed in shame. "It's taken years of work to grow up, to learn healthy ways to be angry, to build a new life far away. And then my dad dies, and I have to deal with my mother again, and all my hard work comes to nothing."

"I wouldn't say that," said Garrett. "I'd say you've been only human under very difficult circumstances."

Jill gave a shred of a smile. "I wish I had your ability to lock down emotionally."

"It's how I survive." Garrett stubbed out his cigarette and turned toward her. "Will you take a walk with me?"

"Sure."

They walked along the salted edge of the driveway past

the gates, and then through the fresh snow on the sidewalk. Garrett halted before the twisted silver maple.

"Do you remember this tree?"

"Yes, but it's not the same. Something's wrong with it."

"I'm wrong with it. I came around this curve too fast one night years ago, drunk, and I hit the tree and knocked it back like this."

"How fast were you going?" asked Jill, awed.

"I don't know. I don't remember anything about it. I must have hit it hard, to push over a tree that massive."

"How come you weren't killed?"

"I don't know."

"Did you go to jail?"

"I went to rehab."

They turned back up the driveway toward the house.

"Mother ought to take that tree down," said Jill.

"She won't," said Garrett. "It's an object lesson about drunk driving. Look, children, what could happen to you if you end up like Garrett French."

"You haven't ended up all that badly," Jill objected. "You've got a real estate empire. You can afford property, which is more than a lot of people can do."

"Thank goodness for dad's money."

"He trusts you with it."

"He's dead."

Jill started to say something and remembered that Mother had made a remark to Garrett about a father's legacy. She shut her mouth.

They reached the porch, and she fished slowly for the front door key in her purse. She had not said anything right all evening, and Garrett, for all his lock on his emotions, seemed as if he very much needed someone to say something right to him.

"You haven't ended up all that badly," she repeated, reaching for something that might spark the same flash of warmth she'd seen so briefly in his face the other day. "And anyway, you're not finished yet."

"Call no man happy until he is dead," Garrett quoted dispassionately.

Jill gave a short laugh of frustration at his utter detachment. "Do you always think so long-term?"

"No," he said. "For example, I notice that you don't have mistletoe in your hair anymore."

And he bid her goodnight and walked toward the parking lot before she could decide how to respond.

Entering the empty house, she found Mother's antique side table still standing in the middle of the hall. If she called him back to help her move it, they would be under the mistletoe, and she would see the lean, tired resignation in his face flicker into something hungry and alive. Maybe if he touched her, she would warm up and the tension in her muscles would melt away. And some short-term happiness might ensue, for them both.

At the open door she stopped short for the second time that day—halted this time not by the sight of Garrett on the mat, but by the distant silhouette of the silver maple leaning drunkenly against the light of a streetlamp, Mother's monument to his alcoholism. A weariness descended over her as she shut the door and responsibly pushed the table back into place. She would not do that to him, she told herself as she climbed the stairs to bed. She would not kiss him on Mother's property.

CHAPTER 5

BEFORE SHE LEFT LOS ANGELES, JILL WENT ON A
whirlwind shopping expedition for a new pair of boots.
She wanted something fun and sexy, something to make
folks at home jealous that they hadn't left Ohio and
become West Coast fashionistas. A tall leather pair, lined
with flannel, little bit of a heel, beckoned to her from a
shop window. They were a splurge, but Jill was in the
mood for some retail therapy.

Those boots were what she should have been wearing
today, to visit Heath at the garage. But she had been
defeated by the weather. The old-timers shook their heads
and said that there had never been such a December for
snow. It was slushy, dirty, and deep. And it was cold. The
first day Jill wore her boots outside, her toes were chilly.
The second time, they'd been numb. After the gift
exchange and her walk with Garrett, she'd peeled off the
boots and spent twenty minutes soaking the blocks of ice
that had been her feet. Today, older and wiser, she wore an
old pair of Del's boots, found on Mother's back porch.

They weren't fun, and they sure as hell weren't sexy, but they were warm, and not much could ruin them.

Anyway, why should she care what Heath thought was sexy? He was a married man, for God's sake. It wasn't as if she wanted to rekindle their relationship. They'd had little enough in common as teenagers, and by now the friendship gap must be unbridgeable. So why would she want him to flirt with her?

Because it's a pulse, she thought, with a flush of shame. It's a sign that I'm still alive and relevant. All these years I've advanced in my career, I've paid my own way, I've given lip service to women's rights and feminist ideals, and yet I don't truly feel like I matter unless a man seems attracted to me. And Heath definitely used to be attracted to me. So maybe if he's not interested now, I don't have it anymore.

But what *did* I have in those days? Heath was mean. He was controlling. And he scared me sometimes. I felt desired, but I never felt loved. We drove each other crazy, in every way. We threw sparks and tantrums. He was a status symbol, the hot edgy guy only I could handle. He used me, and I used him. Oh my God, we were so young. Seventeen and eighteen, driving around town in trucks, drinking beer, having sex that didn't bring us any closer to each other. Where were my parents? Why didn't they put their foot down? And would I have listened if they had? Heath and I never cared what anyone else thought.

We aren't the kind of old friends who just get together. We always wanted something from each other before. What does he want from me now?

And I killed his dog, so that's going to make this a real fun meeting.

. . .

DADDY HAD CHOSEN to build the garage on the edge of town, in a more rough-and-tumble neighborhood. He'd liked the folks there, and they'd liked him. As Jill pulled into the parking lot, the first thing she noticed was that the building had been well maintained, even improved. It wasn't fancy or state-of-the-art, but unlike the Luxembourg Inn, it looked as though someone cared for it.

Jill was prepared for Heath to look as he did at eighteen, in a mechanic's coverall, grease under his nails, with a day or two of stubble on his chin and sweat glistening on his biceps. But the 30-year-old Heath who opened the door to her was freshly shaven, dressed in a managerial sweater and khakis, with his curly hair slicked neatly in place. He greeted her with professional courtesy and offered to make her coffee.

Jill accepted to be polite, though she didn't really want a cup of gas station sludge. To her surprise, however, the waiting room had a Keurig machine and a mini-fridge stocked with bottled water.

"The shop looks great," she said, remembering the old days of folding chairs and a dusty water cooler. "I wouldn't mind sitting here for a few hours while you changed all my tires."

Heath lit up. "That's exactly what I'm going for," he said, presenting her with a steaming cup. "I want my customers to feel at home. They shouldn't be complaining about the waiting room right off the bat."

Jill took a sip and raised her eyebrows. "They won't be able to complain about the java, at any rate. This is gourmet. Three flavors of creamer, even. I hope you're getting a return on your coffee investment."

"Sure." Heath ushered her to a padded chair and paced

the room as if it were a stage. "Look, say that money's tight, you have a lousy job, it's your week with the kids, and your car starts acting up. Where do you go—the dirt-cheap, bare-bones cinder block garage, or my place with free coffee and comfy chairs and the little table with activities that might occupy your kids while you look at your phone in peace for a minute? When people feel valued, that builds loyalty."

"Okay, you've converted me," said Jill, caught off guard by his earnestness. "This is a new side of you—the big-hearted businessman."

"It isn't new," said Heath, refusing to be teased. "It's been a long time since we saw each other. I'm not the same person I was when ..."

"When I killed your dog."

"Oh my God," Heath said, blanching. He passed his hand over his eyes.

Years of therapy to practice thinking about what she was going to say before she said it, all thrown out the window. Why did she need to bring that up out of the blue? Was it a need to throw stuff at Heath, an old relationship habit? Was it a defense mechanism because she thought he might want to get too close while reciting his business model?

Abruptly, Heath asked, "Would you mind stepping into the office?"

Jill felt a little shaky as she followed him into the room Daddy used to sit in, doing accounts. For years she'd imagined what she'd finally tell Heath Albany when she had the chance—about his immaturity, his controlling nature. She'd wanted to hurt him as he'd hurt her. Now she'd brought up old wounds without even meaning to, blurting things out with no self-control, and all her carefully rehearsed phrases were slipping away in the face of the man himself.

She sat in Daddy's swivel chair with the velvet cushion and watched him close the door and settle himself stiffly across the desk from her.

"I can't blame you for still being angry about that dog," he said. "I had hoped ... I'd wanted to move on and just forget about it, but that's not really fair to you."

"I'm not angry, I think," she said, startled by his sincerity. "I didn't mean to bring it up like that. You know how I just say stuff without thinking. I know you loved that dog ..."

"I was scared of that dog," said Heath, looking at his hands clutched in his lap. "I thought it made me intimidating to have this big unmanageable animal. I didn't know how to train him or handle him. I thought it was funny that you would hide behind me when he was around. When I was upset because you were going away, I wanted you to feel threatened by him. And when he charged you, I was terrified, because I didn't know how to stop him."

"But I ran him over," protested Jill, clasping her hands tightly to hold down the tremors that were part and parcel of every stressful conversation these days. "I murdered him, because I hated him. I wanted to show you."

"He attacked you, Jill." Heath finally looked up. He was on the verge of tears. "I was honestly afraid he'd kill you."

Jill flashed back to the moment when she stood in Heath's front yard and screamed that she was leaving, and the dog pushed out of the door and charged at her. She felt the adrenaline rush as she sprinted for the truck and slammed the door on the snarling jaws snapping at her heels. She jammed the key in the ignition and rocketed forward, catching the beast under her wheels. And then, horrified, she'd lurched back and felt the nauseating thump a second time. Heath was yelling her name, but in her memory's newly attuned ear, the rage in his voice transposed itself into terror.

Heath wilted before her now. The last vestiges of the smoldering teenage boy melted away, leaving a middle-aged man weighted with regrets and responsibilities. He was someone else's husband and father.

"I go to church now," he was saying, his voice as ragged as his face. "I've been saved, I've accepted Jesus's forgiveness. But it's hard for me to believe it sometimes. It's hard for me to shake the burden of all the ways I've hurt people over the years. I stand in front of the mirror, and I can barely look at myself. I used to think that nothing I did could ever have consequences I couldn't handle. I was wrong, Jill. I was so wrong."

It should have been gratifying to hear Heath grovel after all these years. Instead, she was left raw and defenseless in the face of his confounding brokenness.

"I'm sorry, Jill. I've needed to tell you that for years. I was a bad person for you to date—for any girl to date. I have a daughter now. I think about how I'd feel if she met someone as screwed up and violent as I used to be, and I feel sick. If I were a better man, I'd have understood that a long time ago, but sometimes you just can't see yourself clearly until a kid sees you." He was crying now. "I pushed you too hard because I wanted to control something. I couldn't control myself."

Jill had her hand over her mouth, but she could not hold down her sobs. Heath knelt in front of her and put his arms around her, as Daddy might have done. "I'm sorry," he wept as he rocked her. "I'm so sorry. Please forgive me."

After a moment she felt herself able to breathe again, and her back was starting to seize up from the awkward position. She gently pushed Heath away and retreated to the bathroom to wash her face. In the harsh fluorescent light, she considered the puffy eyes and blotchy cheeks facing her in the mirror. Could she see the person she used to be? Could she see herself as she was now? Was there any continuity between all the Jills she'd ever been? What did this unfamiliar, humble Heath want from her, and did she have anything left to give him?

When she came out, he was standing behind the desk again, nudging some papers around. "I'm guessing," he said, with a stab at lightness, "that you're not going to be interested in talking about selling me the garage."

"What? Yes! Of course I want to talk about that." Jill took in the carefully arranged papers and Heath's business casual attire, and her perspective on the whole encounter flipped and came to rest upside down. "Is that why you wanted to see me?"

"Yes." Heath squirmed like a little boy caught out in his schemes. "But we don't have to do it now. I can understand if you still hate me. Maybe with our history, it's only fair if you don't want me to get your Dad's garage."

"Stop right there." Jill grabbed a tissue from the box on the desk and blew her nose with purpose. "Look, I know we had a dysfunctional relationship as teenagers. But I don't hate you. And even if I did, I've spent most of the past twelve years valuing businesses. I think I can be professional about this. It's what I do."

Heath took a moment to grapple with their changing dynamic. "You *want* to do business with me?"

"Business is what I do."

He sat back in his chair and breathed out the tension from his shoulders and face. Then he laughed, an unsteady, relieved, joyful sound. Jill realized he'd been nervous about this meeting too. It hadn't been open-ended for him as it was for her. He'd known what he wanted, but couldn't be sure that she would be willing to sit down at the table with him.

"I loved working for your dad," said Heath. "I know he was a little dirty with the accounting, but he had a head for the books and the management and the human side. I'm not any good at the accounts. I need someone to run that side for me."

"Have you talked to my mother about hiring someone?"

Heath became very cautious. "Your mother is ... not a businesswoman. I had a hard time making her understand how I needed to manage the garage."

Jill was nonplussed. "But Mother has run the hotel for years. That's a very complex business."

"Yes," Heath allowed. "But she's not easy to negotiate with. I would never feel secure knowing that she had final authority over my decisions about the garage. I can't talk business with her the way I could with your dad, or like you and I are doing now. Everything is so personal with her."

That was the second time this week that Jill had heard this assessment of Mother. It was true. Mother tore down the things she was trying hardest to preserve. Naturally

Heath would want to be free to run the garage his way, without her trying to interfere.

"Now I think I've got the financing secured," he was saying, fishing papers out of a file and lining them up neatly for her inspection. The meeting became a brisk and professional discussion, two colleagues developing a mutual strategy.

The shop door opened, and little voices called for Daddy. Heath brightened.

"It's Angie and the kids," he said. "Come on, I'll introduce you."

Angie was a forceful woman in scrubs, managing Happy Meals for the two children hanging on her legs. "Daddy, you take Jaxon," she said, thrusting the boy at Heath. "Make sure he eats his dinner. They're so wound up after school," she explained to Jill. "It gets to be dinner time, and I can't settle them down long enough to eat anything. Hon, I've told you before that you have to put the straw in the milk. When you just give him the open carton, he spills it all over."

"I want screen time," fussed the little girl, slightly older than Jaxon. "Mommy, you said I could have screen time."

"After dinner, honey," said Heath, balancing Jaxon on his knee as he scrubbed him with napkins.

"No, Heath, we've discussed this. Jayden is not having screen time until she's checked everything on her chore chart. We have to have a checklist," Angie explained again to Jill, who was edging toward the shop door. "That way everyone knows what I need from them when. Hon, I just said no screen time. Don't let her take your phone."

Jill had never spent much time around small kids. She

didn't know if the fussing now was normal, or was the result of a long day, or of spoiled children, or what. It wasn't her problem to deal with, thank God.

"I'd better go," she said, preparing to make her escape. "I don't want to interrupt your family time."

"Here, let me gather up that paperwork for you," said Heath. He stepped into the office. Jill stood awkwardly with Angie and watched the kids bicker over their chicken nuggets.

"I'm really glad to meet you," said Jill, which was mostly true. "Your kids are adorable."

"They're spoiled rotten," said Angie. "All these electronics, you know? Screens in the car, tablets. I told Heath I didn't want a TV in this waiting room. That's one place the kids aren't going to be sitting in front of a screen. Then he goes and lets them play with his phone."

"I guess it's hard work to raise kids," ventured Jill.

"Heath is a good father," said Angie, a lioness defending her mate. "He works hard so that I only have to be part-time. Lots of men out there wouldn't care who watched the kids, as long as their ladies were bringing in money. I know you only knew him in high school, so you've never seen how much he loves us. The kids are his life."

"I believe it," said Jill, fervently wishing to be anywhere but here. "You guys have a lovely family."

She repeated that to Heath as she stood by the car with him. "Your family is lovely. I'm glad I could get to know them."

"Angie really wanted to meet you," said Heath, eager for her approval. "I know she can be kind of intense. I hope you didn't get the idea she didn't like you." Jill had felt that way, but she was willing to credit Heath's superior knowledge of his own wife. "She's about to go on a twelve-hour shift, so she's a little stressed. There are administration problems at the hospital, and they're always short-staffed, and she has this one co-worker who's always pulling passive-aggressive bullshit ..."

He would have gone on, detailing to Jill the dramas that affected his life intimately and hers not at all, but she took the file from him.

"I'm so glad you're doing well," she said, and she meant it. "Merry Christmas. Give your family my best."

"Yours too," said Heath, opening the car door for her. "Hope your holidays are peaceful."

They would not be, but she accepted the thought in the spirit in which it was given.

CHAPTER 6

EVERYTHING IS SO PERSONAL WITH HER.

Every disagreement must be personal.

As Jill drove back to the Inn, she pondered how Heath Albany and Garrett French, two very different men, had given almost identical assessments of her mother. Heath's was vaguer, which was in character for a man who had rarely lived the examined life. Garrett's analysis was more honed, if limited. He'd never had an agreement with Mother, or he would have known that agreement was also personal with her.

Staying in Mother's good graces required agreeing with her, in the particular way that Mother wanted to be agreed with. For most of her teenage years, Jill fought to stay out of Mother's good graces. Argument had been an act of resistance, the most vital way to assert her sense of self. Even after all these years, as she looked back on the damage that approach had done to her family relationships, she still had a knee-jerk desire to push back at anything Mother wanted to do. She wanted to make disagreement personal.

Well, not this time. She was an adult, here on business that was the very definition of adulting: figuring out the finances, saving the business. If the Luxembourg Inn could be kept in the family, she would keep it in the family. But it seemed more and more like the only way to save the Inn itself would be to sell it, and selling it was going to be tricky if she didn't get the books cleaned up, and soon. It would be helpful if Mother could adult right alongside her, without getting defensive when Jill asked questions. But the only thing Mother could understand about Daddy's whole bookkeeping mess was that he'd done a lot of things under the table, and that was just how you did business.

Daddy's instinct for money was different than Jill's. Jill was good at clarity and bookkeeping. After all, accounting was the only profession in the world where creativity was a crime. But Daddy was creative with his money—not necessarily in a way that was illegal, but that maximized money's potential. Clarity was what Daddy had not wanted. His accounts were a masterful work of redirection. He had a novelistic flair for creating the illusion of a family business scraping by, paying nothing but expenses. If those expenses included all the family cars, Mother's new kitchen, private housekeeping, and agricultural exemptions—which in themselves allowed writing off various pieces of equipment that couldn't be justified by other means—what could a struggling business owner do?

Leave a headache for his accountant daughter, that's what he could do. Oh, Daddy, I wish we had talked about all this while you were still alive.

. . .

THIS WISH WAS ONLY INTENSIFIED as she sat in her mother's office at the Inn.

"Why didn't Daddy create a trust?" Jill asked, as Mother sat at the computer, watching the feeds from the security cameras. "That would have saved us some of these tax woes."

"Because he didn't think he was going to die, of course," said Mother. "Maria at the front desk is doing her online shopping on the registration computer. She doesn't know I can see her. When I've documented ten hours of it, I'm going to fire her."

"Why don't you just talk to her now and give her a warning? Do you have a policy on personal internet use during work hours?"

"I shouldn't have to give her a warning. Employees of the Luxembourg Inn ought to hold themselves to a higher standard."

"Higher than what?" Jill asked. "The Motel 6 by the highway?"

"Jill, it never fails to disappoint me how uncommitted you are to our family traditions of excellence. We strive to uphold your father's legacy here, and all you want to do is to mock." Mother pursed her lips and scrutinized the screen.

This was too pompous a piece of manipulation to be worth getting angry over. Perhaps Mother really was losing her touch. In the old days, one of her sermons would have had fewer buzzwords and a much cleaner evisceration. This was almost too ridiculous to be worth deflecting.

Still, Jill was working up a comeback, just to keep in practice, when Mother's face contorted with genuine anger. She exclaimed at her security feeds and rushed out into the lobby. At the sound of her raised voice, Jill jumped up and followed.

Mother was berating a young employee setting up a ladder by the tree.

"Tell me what you think you're doing," she demanded of the startled girl. "How dare you mess with my Christmas tree? I've chosen the precise position of every ornament on here. Each one is significant. Every year, year after year, I put them in the same places. Perhaps you aren't aware of our tradition? Or maybe tradition isn't important to you?"

"But ma'am," the girl protested meekly, "what about this box of ornaments? I found it in the storage room. I just thought I'd put them on the tree ..."

"You just thought." Mother's voice became deceptively gentle. "You just thought you'd fix my design? You just thought you'd take it on yourself to improve my lobby?"

"No, ma'am, I was only ..."

"Here's what I want you to do. I want you to get off this ladder. I want you to walk out those doors. I want you to go home."

"Oh, ma'am, please don't fire me," the girl begged, her voice beginning to break. "I really need this job. Please ..."

"Who said anything about firing? I want you to go home for the rest of the day and consider whether the Luxembourg Inn is the right place for you to be working, if you can't follow simple procedures."

Weeping now, the girl left.

"Mother, can I talk to you in your office?" asked Jill, appalled.

"No, you may not," said Mother. "I am going home. I am worn out, Jill, worn out with responsibilities and with trying to maintain a standard of hospitality that no one else seems to care about. I wonder why I still work so hard when my friends have all retired to Florida."

"Mother, you cannot speak to employees like that, especially when ..."

"I cannot?" Mother wrapped herself in her coat as in a royal mantle. "I own this place. I can do whatever I want."

The queen of Luxembourg swept out the doors into the swirling snow. An icy wind whistled into the lobby as her figure receded into the unkind elements.

Jill leaned her head against the ladder and contemplated the box of ornaments still sitting on one of the steps. Such a little thing—a box of baubles, almost worthless, and yet to Mother they were a gauntlet thrown down. Heath was right about not being able to talk business with Mother. How could anyone run a shop with the prospect of a harpy hanging over his head?

Jill opened the box, and drew a shuddering breath. Tucked in a nest of tissue paper were her father's favorite Christmas ornaments, the ones he'd taken to the garage every year and put on a little tree in the corner of the waiting room. Daddy had not been here this year to bring them out of storage. The ornaments had been alone and forgotten in some cold, dusty corner, like Daddy in his grave ...

She would do it. She would hang those ornaments on the tree, Mother be damned. Daddy was not going to rot forgotten if she could help it. Jill climbed up the waiting ladder and began decking the halls with a vengeance. On this branch, her third-grade picture in a little frame; over here, a crocheted ball Del had made in Scouts; down a bit, a cross-stitched dove in a plastic frame, signed "R" for

Reagan. If she reached out just a bit, she could hang the papier-mâché star right in the center of the tree ...

The ladder tipped dangerously. Jill yelped and flailed, and found herself toppling off, into a pair of steady arms.

"Your Christmas tree is exquisite," said Mr. Singh, gently setting her upright. "But it would be too bad if you were to suffer a broken arm for your art."

"I ... I lost my balance," Jill said unnecessarily. She didn't know which way to look, partly because Mr. Singh was still supporting her, and partly because she could barely see through her tears anyway. A clean handkerchief, evincing the merest suspicion of exotic scent, was pressed into her palm, and firm, cool hands were guiding her to a couch. Jill sat and wept. All she had done on this trip was cry in front of men. What was wrong with her? She never cried in Los Angeles. If Daddy had been here, he would have laughed and called her "Hon" and told Mother exactly where she could hang his ornaments ...

Mr. Singh sat beside her, neither patient nor impatient, neither comforting nor uncomfortable. He made no judgment on the soggy handkerchief she finally handed back to him, nor did he offer it to her to keep, which men generally did in movies, but tucked it back in his pocket as if it were no different than before. Nothing seemed to faze him, not women tumbling from trees, not torrents of hysterics, not Jill babbling about Daddy and the bookkeeping and everything that had been weighing on her all month.

"You have been juggling many balls," said Mr. Singh. "The hotel, the garage, the ag exemption ... And may I ask what an ag exemption is?"

Jill gave a damp snort of laughter. "It was one of

Daddy's little cheats. He owned a piece of land down by the highway, and he put some cows to graze on it to get an agricultural exemption on his taxes, and ... oh, it's all so silly. Why do we hold onto these things that do us no good? Daddy inherited that land. Mother doesn't want it. It's useless for farming, and it's not near anything. And yet Daddy would never sell it, because it was his. And Mother won't sell it, because it was his legacy. And I'm putting up Christmas ornaments to honor Daddy's legacy. We keep throwing the word around, but I don't even know what it means. I know the legal definition, but in my case, what is Daddy's legacy?"

"A legacy is a gift from the past to the present," said Mr. Singh. "Do you believe that all these things your father has left you are his gifts to you?"

"No," said Jill, pondering. "No, the hotel, the garage ... these are just things. Daddy worked hard to keep them running, but if they have any worth in themselves, then someone else should be able to run them now that he's gone. What I treasure most is his love, what he taught me about life. That's what I would want to pass on. I would want to honor the person that he was, not just the stuff he handed on."

Mr. Singh sighed. "Those who have children to carry on their memories are blessed indeed. A child preserves, remembers, endures." He paused, his perfect face graven with human lines of sadness. "My father had a sister who died young. She was murdered by a man because she would not marry him. My aunt was beautiful and well-loved, and many vowed to fight for justice for her and carry on in her name. But that was fifty years ago. Who remembers her now? She died years before I was born. She had no children to keep her memory fresh, to protest when her murderer was released from prison. When my father dies, there will be no one on earth who has touched my aunt. I can visit her tomb and pray for justice, but her legacy died out before it was established."

Although he had not moved any nearer to her, his formality seemed more intimate than if he were whispering in her ear. Jill had never thought of herself as incomplete without children, but something in Mr. Singh's voice released whatever gear of her biological clock had been frozen in place. Face flushed, lips parted, her whole being was drawn toward him, toward their glorious union that would culminate in a passel of beautiful, deep-eyed, gently scented children. She was almost drooling at the thought ...

She was drooling, literally. Hastily, she shut her mouth and wiped her face. Mr. Singh seemed to find nothing remarkable in her behavior, and indeed, she had been soppy enough today that one more bit of facial fluid could hardly seem surprising. Jill swallowed hard to clear her throat and restore her wits.

"I am so sorry for your loss," she said at last, foolishly, reaching for a way to honor his forgotten aunt.

"And I for yours," he said, standing. When she took his offered hand, he pulled her to her feet. "May your burdens be lightened soon." And then he disappeared to the regions whence he came, leaving Jill to calm her racing pulse with deep breaths of the lightly spiced air.

CHAPTER 7

CHRISTMAS IN A SMALL TOWN! EVERYWHERE YOU LOOK
and listen, the sights and sounds of the season fill the
heart with cheer. Front porches twinkling a welcome.
Wreaths on the streetlamps. Tinsel in the shop windows.
Carolers muffled in woolen scarves.

And the Holiday Dance Recital.

The auditorium of Luxembourg High School teemed
with milling family members trying to find blocks of seats
to accommodate their bodies, coats, and tributes of flowers. Through the press, Jill saw Reagan waving her down to
the front row.

"Is it okay to sit here?" Jill asked.

"I've saved the whole row," said Reagan, moving to
intercept a white-haired lady moving into O'Leary territory. "Excuse me, ma'am, these seats are reserved."

"I don't see anyone sitting here," said the lady,
preparing to get comfortable.

"I've got my coat on the last seat," said Reagan sweetly.
"I'm sorry, but you'll have to move." To Jill, she said, "You

take the seat on the end and don't let anyone but our group past."

"Who's 'our group'?" Jill asked, but Reagan had already moved to the end of the row and was chatting with some other dance moms. Heath and Angie were sitting in the section across the aisle from Reagan, with family who'd come out in force to cheer little Jayden at her first recital. Turning around, Jill almost yelped to find Mr. Singh at her elbow, abrupt and mysterious as Herr Drosselmeier. He bowed as he passed down the aisle to take a place by Reagan. Del arrived just after him, shadowed by her husband. They sat near Jill's end of the row.

"We always leave the center seat for Mother," Del said.

"Nothing but the best for Mother," Jill sniped. "God forbid she should have anything less. Do you know she almost fired a girl today for trying to put Daddy's old ornaments from the garage on the tree at the Inn? Wouldn't do to have Daddy's ratty stuff cluttering up Mother's decorating scheme."

"Stop being the center of your own universe," said Del, unperturbed. "You're not the only one grieving Dad."

"What is that supposed to mean?"

"Just because Mother is a manipulative bitch doesn't mean she didn't love Daddy. Her grief comes out in grasping at control. Being in control feels like stability to her."

Jill opened her mouth to retort, and then shut it. All her life Mother had been a goad, inciting her to animal fury. She had learned to manage her own anger through dint of therapy and patient work, but she'd never considered why it was that Mother was driven to dominate. Now, as if Del had flipped a light switch, Jill understood: if

Mother could find fault with someone else, she didn't have to find fault with herself.

Whereas Mother's first instinct was to control everything, Jill's own first instinct was to blow everything up. And here she had been, about to lash out at Del, without even thinking about what Del had said.

"Wow," she breathed, on the verge of a great insight. "Mother and I have completely opposite ways of dealing with frustration."

"Yes," said Del, as one would address a particularly bright kindergartener.

When Mother came, Jill let her past without a murmur.

"Can I sit here?" asked a woman holding an oversized bouquet, trying to edge into the empty seat next to Jill.

"I'm sorry, this seat's taken," said Jill. She had just spied Garrett French standing awkwardly in the back, the only dark face in the crowd. As the lady huffed off, Garrett noticed Jill's tentative wave and crossed the auditorium with the relief of a man who has just caught hold of a life preserver.

"Thank you so much," he said as she scooted over to give him the aisle seat. "I've never been to a dance recital before. I don't know the protocol."

"It's my first too," Jill said. "But you can't be here to see Quennedey."

"My niece wanted me to come see her dance," he said, turning over the program with its interminable list of Olivias and Lilys and Avas.

"Can you not find your family?" Jill asked. She helpfully scanned the room although she had no idea who she was looking for. No one resembled Garrett.

"I know exactly where my brother is," Garrett said shortly. "I just couldn't bear the thought of sitting with him for an hour."

The lights dimmed, leaving Jill to wonder whether the set of his mouth was defiance or shame.

"Good evening, ladies and gentlemen!" A cheery voice blared through the speakers, begging them to enjoy the show and to remember that since it was already being recorded, there was no need for anyone to take video of the dances. "Please give your dancer all your attention and leave the filming to us!"

The curtain rose on a trio of blondes in unitards writhing mostly in sync. Jill didn't know much about dancing, but she thought if she had been paying out for dance classes only to discover that her child was doing a lyrical interpretation of Pentatonix's "The Little Drummer Boy," she would have asked for her money back. Fortunately, Jayden Albany and the Wee Dance ballet class, up next, were adorable in their tutus. The Tiny Tappers got confused and spent most of their dance waving to their mothers, but the Hip-Hopsters had a boy who had an actual sense of rhythm.

The key to surviving a dance recital, it seemed, was to pick out one talented child in each class and watch her throughout the number. It helped that the kids were cute and the costumes pretty. Every now and then there was the pleasing novelty of a dance that was worth watching for its own sake. The advanced Tap class did a surprisingly deft routine to a bluegrass version of "What Child Is This," which Jill and Garrett agreed justified the price of the tickets. But most of the dances were notable only to parents or grandparents, who could be picked out of a crowd because they all had their phones out, recording.

The pointe class was up next, and Reagan was explaining to Mr. Singh how Quennedey was the youngest dancer, and how she'd had to be granted special permission to join the class early.

"She's spent hours working on her showcase solo," said Reagan, sighing over a life dedicated to the arts. "She hasn't even let me see it. She's such a perfectionist."

The ballerinas shuffled out *en pointe* and set their positions. Quennedey looked a bit sullen next to the older girls, but when the music started, she seemed competent enough on her toes. Reagan preened.

"The solos are coming up," she whispered, adjusting the focus on her phone.

One by one, the girls stepped forward and performed sixteen counts of plies and spins and arabesques. Jill wondered if Reagan's running commentary on the class dramas was supposed to be part of her video. Now Quennedey was up. She posed, grinned, and broke into a vigorous Hype. The audience roared its approval.

"What?" gasped Reagan, as Quennedey Flossed double-time.

"Stop," she moaned as Quennedey did a gritty Orange Justice.

"No," she barked, as Quennedey ended with a crisp Dab.

The luckless dancers soloing after Quennedey were entirely thrown off and stumbled through their choreography. Reagan foamed at the mouth. Next to Jill, Del nodded.

"Did you know she was going to do that?" Jill whispered.

"I could have told you she was going to do that," Del replied. "Why would anyone expect anything else?"

IT WAS an evening of traditions that were new to Jill. "Quennedey's Dance Recital" turned out to be more than simply the recital. It was the dancing, and the traditional dinner at Gino's afterward, and the traditional watching of the video back at Mother's house after that. Why it was necessary to watch a video of a recital they'd all just seen in person was unclear to Jill. Perhaps it wouldn't make sense to her until she had kids of her own—a phrase that both Mother and Reagan had used on her several times during the week.

"You'll love Gino's!" Reagan gushed as they waited for their table. "It's authentic Italian. You can't get real home-town quality from a chain."

Jill was ready to appreciate some good Italian and some good wine. An isolation was stealing over her, only amplified by the biological clock Mr. Singh had set ticking. He was here at the family dinner, attending upon Reagan and Quennedey with impersonal courtliness. Reagan basked in the reflected glory of having both a man and a child in her train. Del and her little husband—what was his name? Scott?—sat cozily in a corner, discussing whatever it was they discussed. And Mother, of course, had all her descendants dancing attendance on her, and didn't she know it.

Only Jill was solo, without partner or prospect. That didn't matter so much in Los Angeles. She had friends there, and at the office no one cared that she was the middle child, so long as she did her work competently. Now, back in the bosom of her family, she seemed never to have left. Twelve years of independence, of college, of professional certification, of successful career, and she might as well still be a rebellious eighteen-year-old, for all the weight anyone gave her opinions or her expertise. No, I didn't act like an adult then! she wanted to shout. But I'm acting like an adult now, here, in this town, at this restaurant, by myself.

AN HOUR EARLIER, as the falling action had dragged on after the recital—flowers, photos, dressing, packing up the costume and make-up—Jill stood alone in the auditorium, an island among a teeming sea of families and friends. Then Garrett, who'd slipped off during the bows and interminable announcements, reappeared at her side.

"Did you find your niece?" she asked.

"She's over there," he said. Jill followed his gaze over to a petite blonde ballerina held by a bulky blue-eyed man with a beard like an Amish farmer. As they saw Garrett looking at them, they both waved, and he nodded back.

"That's your brother?" Jill asked, trying not to sound surprised.

"We don't have the same mother," said Garrett briefly. "I didn't go out to see them. I needed a smoke break."

"Take me with you next time."

"For a smoke?"

"For the break."

They waited together while the other O'Learys made the social rounds, and while they waited, they talked. Jill found herself pouring out what had been consuming most of her days: the accounting, the taxes, the valuations, even Heath and the garage. She laid out the case that the Inn was more profitable than it looked on paper, based on the real expenses instead of the padded profit-and-loss statements with which Daddy had warded off the tax man. And this villainous investor, Mother's arch-nemesis, asked intelligent questions, and comprehended the scale of the task she'd undertaken, and accepted that she was a professional. He responded to her not on Mother's terms, but on her own. By the time the others were ready to leave, he'd agreed that he needed to raise his offer for the Inn.

"Would you like to keep discussing this over dinner?" he asked.

She did want to, very much. At least, she wanted the dinner with him. But she had already committed to go to Gino's with her family. She felt her chance of real conversation slipping away, and with it, somehow, her very self. Suddenly her loneliness was intolerable.

"We're all going back to my mother's house afterward to watch the recital video," she said, in a rush. "I know it's awkward for you there, but at least there are snacks and drinks and plenty of rooms and nooks for conversations. That way I'd be at the family event, which will keep the peace, but we could still talk. It can't be too exclusive a party. Mr. Singh will be there."

"The dark horse," said Garrett, eyeing Mr. Singh waiting courteously on Reagan. "What is he playing for, I wonder?"

"Maybe he loves small town life." Jill snickered.

"Maybe he loves watching dance recitals," Garrett sniggered.

"Maybe he loves Reagan," Jill almost howled. They would have collapsed on each other in giggles if the possibility of brushing against his cheek with her own had not quickly sobered her up.

Jill felt herself duty-bound to check on Reagan and make sure she would neither die of apoplexy nor strangle her daughter. But Reagan had put aside thoughts of violence. Mr. Singh praised Quennedy's dance and said it was quite in keeping with the finest traditions of Bollywood.

"Even Misty Copeland cannot master those moves," he said.

"He's seen her try?" murmured Garrett in Jill's ear. She snorted.

"I have," said Mr. Singh, and he bowed his bow to them both as he escorted Reagan and a dozen roses to wait by the dressing rooms for the young ballerina.

But at the restaurant, without Garrett to distract her, she observed Mr. Singh with a keen eye. If he was bored with Quennedey, he hid it well. Quennedey warmed to the attention, talking too loudly about herself.

"I was almost rich," she bragged, between gulps of a noxious neon soda. "Grandpa was going to give me some land for my college fund. But I don't want to go to college. College is for the elite."

"You would like to live on this land?" Mr. Singh asked.

"My mom talks about building a house on it, if she can get Grandma to give it to her," said Quennedey. "But I don't think my mom will ever get around to it. She needs a man to take care of all that stuff for her."

"Your mother seems more than competent to me, and I have no doubt she can make wise decisions on her own," said Mr. Singh, gracing Reagan with a judicious smile. Reagan oozed all over the place.

"There, Jill, what did we tell you?" said Mother, pawing through the bread basket. "Isn't Gino's divine? We just scarf these breadsticks. Gino bakes them himself."

Jill, who had been to high-end trattorias in Los Angeles, could believe that Gino's culinary skills extended even to the baking of frozen breadsticks. Everything around her —the basic pasta, the undistinguished marinara, the food-service ingredients, the house red, the family content with a facsimile of good food—suddenly pressed in. The creeping loneliness seized her again, and only the thought of seeing Garrett later in the evening gave her the warmth she needed to smile or speak or breathe.

CHAPTER 8

JILL SHOULD HAVE KNOWN THAT A SCENE WAS COMING. All through dinner Mother consumed the attentions of her family, feeding on Reagan's flatteries and Del's smackdowns with vampiric relish. What did not please her was Jill's silence. Mother couldn't bear being ignored, and there was never any telling how far she might push to get a reaction. Even Del's Teflon nerves seemed frayed by the time everyone settled down at the house to watch the recital, again.

With sufficient care and duty, the scene might have been avoided. Or perhaps not. All Jill's work of the past weeks had gone into preventing future strife, but Mother was spoiling for a showdown now. And as unkind fortune would have it, Mother was the one nearest the front door when the bell rang. She opened it to find that lowdown Garrett French on her own doorstep.

"Hello, Regina," said Garrett, knocking the snow from his boots. "Jill asked me over."

"Did she indeed?" said Regina, unmoved in the doorway. "Is this Jill's house now, that she invites people here without even consulting me?"

Jill dashed down the stairs, cursing her stupid vanity. All she'd wanted to do was check her hair and makeup, to make sure she hit the golden mean between Del's austerity and Reagan's excess. She ought to have mentioned to Mother that Garrett was coming over, of course. But it was a rich, rare thing to be able to anticipate anything these days, and she hadn't wanted to mar her fortune with Mother's displeasure.

"I'm sorry, Mother," she said, pulling the door all the way open. "I thought it would be nicer if I didn't have to leave the house. That way I'm still spending time with the family."

"If you're talking to Garrett French, you won't be spending time with our family," said Regina, turning and walking down the hall.

"You don't mind?" Jill asked Garrett in a low voice, hanging up his coat. "We could go out somewhere, I guess."

"In Luxembourg? Not much open this time of night. Unless you want to come over to my place." He saw the ball of mistletoe overhead. "But I like it here just fine."

They stood, under the mistletoe, not quite looking at one another. Jill's thoughts raced from chance to chance. Should she take a step closer? Was he waiting for a sign from her? Did this mean anything at all? Slow down, lady —you've only known this man for two weeks, if that.

"If you're going to kiss, go ahead and do it," said Del from behind them. "But could you not block the bathroom door?"

Jill nudged Garrett into Daddy's office and shut the door.

"Maybe we can talk in here," she was saying, when a sleepy head rose over the back of the couch.

"My mom said you two should get a room," Quennedey mumbled, rubbing her eyes. "Are you getting this room? Are you going to kiss? Can I watch?"

"Go back to sleep," said Jill, beating a hasty retreat.

Garrett lingered in the doorway of the kitchen while Jill went in to find drinks that weren't wine or beer.

"The lady of the house herself," drawled Mother. "Help yourself to anything. No need to ask me."

"Thank you, Mother," said Jill with clenched jaw.

Down a step in the den, everyone was gathered to ignore the dance recital on the screen. Del, back from the bathroom, sat as always with Scott squished by her side. Reagan wanted to curl up as closely as possible to Mr. Singh but didn't dare encroach on his couch cushion. And there was Mother holding court, a manic gleam in her eye.

"It's so nice to have a house to call your own," she said, with razor-edged charm. "One large enough to host one's daughters and all their guests. Soon I'll be retired, living as a guest in your homes. I hope you'll be gracious if I invite friends without consulting you first."

"I don't see why you can't just retire to Florida like you want to," said Reagan with easy, noncommittal support. "You deserve to relax."

"I do deserve to relax," agreed Mother, in tones of melodramatic weariness that carried all the way to the cheap seats. "But Gillian doesn't seem to think so. I'm tired. I'm alone. I have been juggling all the burdens your father left me, and now I want to lay them down.

But how can I sell the hotel when Gillian says it's worthless?"

"Mother, I don't say that," Jill said, the pattern of patience. She would not let Mother goad her into getting angry. Not in front of Garrett, who understood the work she was doing even if no one else did. If he could shut down emotionally to survive, surely she could too, just for a few minutes. "Everything Daddy left you is worth more than it looks like on paper. It's just a matter of sorting out all the expenses and making a more accurate assessment."

"I should certainly think that everything Daddy left me is worth more than it looks on paper," Mother said, on her dignity. "Daddy loved me. He worked hard to show it. He loved you girls. He wanted to leave you his life's work as your inheritance. I've been trying to maintain his legacy, not for my own benefit—God knows I'm getting little enough out of it—but for you girls, as a sign of my love. Is that worthless?"

Jill, biting her tongue, willed herself to silence. There was no good that could come out from answering this rhetorical question. Mother, however, did not consider it rhetorical. She wheeled on Reagan and demanded, "You tell me, Reagan. Is my love worthless?"

Reagan, caught off guard, rallied herself to worm out of the crosshairs. "Of course not, Mother! You know Jill has some deep-seated need to set us all at odds. But when have I ever acted out that way? I'm your oldest girl. I love you. I love this house. I love the Inn. I love everything you and Daddy built for us." She relaxed into her monologue. "Nothing in my life has ever brought me so much happiness as wandering with Daddy around that old property down by the highway. We used to shoo the cows off the path when we walked down to the creek. It's like my spiritual home. Truth to tell," and here Jill could have sworn that Mr. Singh gave Reagan the smallest nod, "I wish it were my forever home. I've been dreaming about building on that land. I want Daddy's granddaughter to live in the place he loved so much. And I want to make a home for you too, Mother. I want a house big enough for you to live with me when that day comes."

Jill almost choked on her disgust. Daddy's interest in that land had been purely mercenary, and the few times Reagan had been there when they were children, she'd been distinctly, disrespectfully bored. A house for Mother! What safe generosity, since Mother wanted to retire to Florida. Jill wished Mother *would* move in with Reagan. They deserved each other. At least Mother's smackdown of Reagan's crass flattery would be worth watching.

"Darling, it's yours," Mother said, embracing her devoted eldest daughter. "The land should go to someone who loves it. Daddy would be so proud."

"Oh, Mother," Reagan sobbed adorably. "Oh, Mother!"

Her arm around Reagan, Mother extended her other arm to Del. "What about you, Del? What is my love worth to you?"

"Mother, you're full of shit," said Del, unruffled. "And so's Reagan. If she loves that scrubland so much, why doesn't she marry it? I don't need to kiss up to you for your money, and I'm not tied to Ohio. Scott can move his home office anywhere. Quit fishing for compliments. If I didn't love you, I wouldn't be here."

Amazingly, Mother took this in her stride. "That's my

Delly," she murmured, content with tough love from her baby. "Of course, I don't want to be a burden. I'll give you what you want: nothing, and may you be happy with it."

"I am," said Del.

"My girls," Mother breathed. "Here we all are, together again, at Christmas time. Can't we love one another, for Daddy's sake? Oh, darling," and she turned the force of her tenderness on Jill, who had retreated to the doorway where Garrett was standing, "you're so clever. Don't use that against me. Don't punish me for the past by devaluing what Daddy left me to live on. You can't hate me that much."

This last appeal stunned Jill like a blow to the stomach. She hid her icy hands behind her back so that no one could see her fists ready to strike something, anything. Mother was always adept at finding an unarmored chink and shooting her arrow directly into it. How could she know Jill's weakness even after all this time? Could she see the rage still beating in Jill's raw heart?

A madness of motivations raged like a tempest through her mind. Was she such a bad daughter? Was it possible that she was assigning a lower worth to Mother's assets because she wanted to hold power over Mother? She knew all the accounting tricks to make a property seem more valuable on paper, as Daddy had made it seem less valuable on paper. Why couldn't she just love her mother the way her mother wanted to be loved?

Her nails bit into her palms, maybe drawing blood. It would serve her right to bleed. Nothing else could relieve the pressure swelling up toward her heart. What if she screamed at Mother, threw something at her, anything to make her shut up? Or what if she took the easy way out, flattered and cringed and bought Mother's approval? Maybe she could make Mother love her, and that would make up for every time Mother had belittled and manipulated and ignored and humiliated her.

Violence or submission—wasn't there any other path? Already her ears buzzed and her eyes burned with the heat of tears unshed. Quick breaths clamored at her throat. She would collapse in a heap, crying again, the only thing she could do in Ohio, and Mother would win on both fronts.

She felt a hand wrap around her fist, gently coaxing her clenched fingers open. Behind her, Garrett laced his fingers between hers and rubbed some life back into her frozen joints. The unexpected relief only emphasized anger's grip on the rest of her body. She crushed Garrett's hand until she felt him wince. Let him learn what she was really like. He could push her away just like everyone else always did.

Instead, she felt him pull her back into the warmth of his body. The touch of his hand she had resisted, but with this embrace he drew the tension from her aching muscles into himself. She closed her eyes and absorbed his strength. A peace, fresh as rain, dispersed her clouded thoughts, revealing for an instant the vast clarity of the starlit universe.

"I don't hate you, Mother," she said, in a voice steadied by his support. "I love you because you're my mother, and because that's what I'm supposed to do. And that's all I have. Maybe you don't know how hard you were to live with. Maybe you don't realize how you often tore me apart when I was growing up. Maybe you didn't know the damage you did. But I am damaged. I don't hate you, and it's a victory for me even to be able to say that much. I can't give you any more than that."

In the speechless room, Mother drew herself up to an untouchable height.

"Let me give *you* something, Gillian," she said. "My love is worthless to you, so I'll match it with something just as worthless to me. Since I'm not to be allowed to sell the Inn to support myself, it's my gift to you. You're so eager to get back to Los Angeles and leave us all behind to cope with the mess. Now you can cope with it. Now you can have a tie that binds you to your home—a financial tie, the kind you understand."

She strode regally to the doorway, then halted by Garrett.

"There, boy," she said, in a voice sharp as ice. "She has what you want. You can lowball her for it now. Or you can take her for her miserable dowry. It's nothing to me anymore."

"Do not call him 'boy' ever again," Jill spat, gripping Garrett's hand behind her. "I'd rather have his love than yours."

Mother, on the bottom step, turned with tragic grandeur to play out her last line. "To think how pleased I was when you were born, the second child I longed for. And this is how you've turned out—a thankless daughter."

She swept up the stairs, leaving her audience in heavy silence. Jill realized that she would wait in vain for her sisters to take her part, or Garrett's. They were, in their different ways, as beaten down by dealing with Mother as she was. Now they could escape: implacable Del towing Scott, who seemed more anxious about the family strife than his wife was; jittery Reagan hustling a groggy

Quennedey into her coat. Mr. Singh, departing, bowed inscrutably to Jill, or Garrett, or them both as one. Closing her eyes, Jill could hear her sisters in brief whispered conference by the door, but she did not move, and neither did Garrett. For this moment, at least, they were still and secure, holding each other's wounds closed.

CHAPTER 9

THE NEXT DAY JILL MOVED TO THE INN. SHE HAD GONE to bed after the blowup, in shock, numb to everything but the memory of Garrett's protection. But after a bad night she woke up in an incandescent rage. What had she done to merit having her very existence denigrated by her own mother? How dare Mother foist the Inn on her as a punishment? How dare she make accounting a litmus test of love? It was ridiculous to come back to Ohio only to run away from the family house a second time, but Jill was damned if she was going to stay another night under the same roof with Mother, or listen to her make another bigoted crack at Garrett.

Jill didn't put much stock in Mother's threat to transfer ownership of the Inn to her, but as she was checking in at the desk, the manager pleaded for her help. The poor woman wrung her hands as she explained that Mrs. O'Leary refused to come in today. Jill was in charge now, Mrs. O'Leary had said. Jill dismissed this as mere theatrics, but no, it turned out Mother was in earnest. On a day when she desperately needed some quiet time to put her life back together, Jill found herself signing off on purchasing decisions and interviewing new cleaning staff.

In the afternoon she received a call from Reagan.

"Why don't you come over to my place tonight?" Reagan suggested, with a chumminess that put Jill on her guard. "Del and Quennedey and I are going to bake some Christmas cookies, and I thought you might want to join us. You know, have a little sister time."

Jill had had about all the sister time she could stomach, but the underlying note of hysteria in Reagan's voice intrigued her. And so, that evening in Reagan's kitchen, she draped herself in a green apron with a big Rudolph nose pom-pom, sending up clouds of flour as she rolled out cookies.

"I wasn't even 100% serious about building a new house," moaned Reagan, glancing around at the gourmet kitchen financed by alimony. "And now Mother won't get off my case about it. She's been calling me all day with plans and suggestions about how we should lay it out. She's talking to her lawyers about how to transfer the ownership of the Inn. I thought she was serious about wanting to move to Florida."

"She wanted to move to Florida with Daddy," said Del, settling on a stool. She didn't like baking and wasn't even pretending to help. "She's falling apart without him. She depended on him to rein her in. Now that he's gone, she doesn't know how to manage herself."

Quennedey was underfoot, armed with cookie cutters. "Mom said Grandma was off her meds."

Jill didn't feel quite ready to talk about Daddy, or Mother without Daddy. "Why did you even bring up the land last night then?" she snapped at Reagan. "You weren't obligated to say anything."

"You get to go back to Los Angeles. We're stuck living here with Mother," Reagan griped. "What good does it do me to be on her bad side? Anyway, I thought it might be a chance to call dibs on the land."

"Why?" Jill demanded. "You've never cared about it before."

Reagan shrugged elaborately. "Mr. Singh says that owning land is a solid investment."

Jill flattened the dough with a vengeance. "And so you kissed up to Mother and left me holding the bag, just to get a piece of stupid property?"

"Why not?" Reagan demanded in her turn. "What else has Mother ever had to give? Affection? The milk of human kindness? If she can't behave like a human to her children, at least she could give us our inheritance before she completely demolishes it."

"If you roll those cookies any thinner, they're going to burn," said Del. "So, you'll get her to hand you her property, and then you're planning to support her when she retires?"

Reagan blanched. "But she's going to Florida!"

"On what money?" asked Del.

Jill finally let Quennedey shove her away from the dough. "Well, if that money is supposed to come from her properties, I guess it's up to me."

"I'm the only grandchild, so it's all my money in the end," said Quennedey, stamping the cookie cutters into the dough with satisfying thumps.

❄

JILL WAS DETERMINED NOT to do anything underhanded, so she scrutinized the accounts before she felt satisfied that she could afford to call in a consultant. Then she placed a call to Amita Patel.

"Hey, girlfriend, how's snowy Ohio?" chirped Amita.

"Out of control. Even the old-timers can't remember such a horrible year. Want an expenses-paid trip to see it for yourself?"

Amita's enthusiasm carried all the way across three time zones.

"I want to see everything! I want to ride a horse and go sledding and eat chestnuts roasted on an open fire. What about the ex-boyfriend? Is he available? Has he been making your life miserable?"

"Who?" Jill's mental wheels spun for a moment. "Oh, yeah. No, there's no drama there. Heath is the least of my worries."

"Well, all your worries are over now! We'll straighten out your books, and then we're going to make the season merry and bright."

Oh, the season will be bright, Jill thought. That glow is just my family burning down.

AMITA WAS ENCHANTED by everything about Ohio—the flatness, the fields, the snow that fell relentlessly during the drive from Columbus. Jill nodded and smiled, but mainly she concentrated, white-knuckled, on keeping the car on the road. Rural living was charming until you were in a near whiteout, wondering when the next marker of civilization was going to appear, or if you were going to skid and die in a forest ditch in the middle of nowhere.

"So, tell me all about everyone," Amita ordered. "What happened with the ex-boyfriend?"

"Nothing, really. He's a normal guy trying to run a business."

"Anything going on there?"

"He has a wife and two kids. And we don't have anything in common anymore, if we ever did."

Amita deflated. "So much for romance."

"Would you consider my mother's real-estate nemesis an acceptable substitute?" Jill offered. "Emotionally inaccessible, smokes, has father issues and used to be an alcoholic, but is single and easy on the eyes."

"Jill," Amita scolded, fixing her with a stern eye. "This one is a bad bet."

"He's also patient and gentle and he says 'ergo.'"

"Points to him, I guess, but he still sounds kinda sketch to me."

"And then there's our man of mystery, Mr. Singh. Tall, dark, elegant, seems to know everything. Probably royalty. Certainly rich."

Amita was not impressed. "I'd stick with the nemesis. At least he's a real person."

A real person. Amita was right that on paper Garrett sounded dicey. Jill was ashamed of herself for playing up his flaws, but they really were flaws. If she'd heard some other man described that same way, she would have written him off as bad news, not worth the trouble of building a relationship. But Garrett himself, in the fullness of his person, was very good news to Jill. He was more than his past, whatever it was. And he'd seen some fairly flawed sides of Jill herself and hadn't rejected her, yet.

He'd texted the morning after Mother's rampage to

check on her, and they'd exchanged quiet messages on and off since. It was new and strange to be peaceful with someone—not just withdrawn or guarded or civil, but truly pacific. Garrett brought out this hidden quality in her. Was there anything hidden in him that only she could bring out?

There was material for lots of fruitful meditation there, but Amita was pushing onward. "How about your mother? What's going on with her?"

Jill, her bubble of serenity burst, sighed. "How can you talk to someone who's the center of her own universe? Nothing I say is right. But I'm going to finish this job anyway."

"And then? Which of the guys do you pick?"

Jill snorted. "What do you mean, which do I pick? What is this, a Hallmark movie? Why should these men be my only options, simply because they both reside in my hometown at this particular point on the space-time continuum?"

But Amita was an incurable romantic. "Los Angeles is full of men, but you're still single. Maybe you've been subconsciously waiting all these years to come back home."

"You're single, too!"

Amita grinned and extended her arms to embrace the car, the snow, the blurred outlines that indicated that they'd entered the forest. "So, Ohio must work its Christmas magic on me!"

"I'm not sure you understand Ohio, or Christmas, or magic," Jill humphed, but resist as she might, Amita's cheer pierced her gloomy soul.

. . .

Even Amita's indomitable optimism found its Waterloo in the Inn's finances, however. After a long day, she and Jill sat in the Luxembourg Inn's restaurant, nursing mulled wine and tension headaches. Across from them, Garrett resolutely sipped the Inn's signature coffee blend. Mother had insisted that a signature blend gave the Inn cachet. Mother's restaurant-supply company had swindled her. Whatever cachet tasted like, Jill was certain it was better than this.

"You're never going to be able to fix up this place on the profits alone," Amita said, her eyes fixed in gloomy reverie on the gold and avocado carpet. "And it wants fixing up."

Jill sloshed her wine around her mug. "Mother looks at the revenue and says, 'All this money, we're doing fine!' But the revenue is plowed back into expenses, and there's simply not enough profit, even after I've cleaned up the books, to make it possible for us to afford renovations. We'd need a loan for more than five years' worth of profit to even begin to touch the upgrades the Inn needs, and frankly, we're a bad risk for any lender."

"Also, your coffee is terrible," said Garrett. Having no personal or professional stake in the Inn's woes, he could have his little joke.

"If you want better coffee, why don't you invest in the Inn?" snapped Jill, who privately agreed with his assessment.

"I invest in properties that I own," said Garrett. "And your mother doesn't want to sell to me, and you don't technically own the Inn yet."

Jill was about to retort that she wouldn't sell it to him even if she did own it when a faint thrum of music, a breath of Bollywood, seemed to drone in her ear. She blinked and looked around, but she saw nothing out of the ordinary except Mr. Singh, gliding through the lobby toward the carved front doors.

"Mr. Singh," Jill called to him. He turned toward her, probably to bow, but one glance at their table made him pause as if he were under a spell. Jill made a mental note to have all the doors and windows checked: a draft was blowing Amita's hair back from her face. The lights, too, were acting up. The sudden brightness made the colors of the restaurant swim and pop.

"I'd like to introduce you to my friend Amita Patel, from Los Angeles," said Jill hastily, shaking her head to clear it. "She's here to help me with the accounting."

Mr. Singh crossed to their table in slow motion.

"Miss Patel," he said, low and intimate. "I'm enchanted to meet you."

"Mr. Singh," said Amita, with lashes demurely sweeping her cheeks. "The pleasure is all mine."

The light was certainly all wrong. The lamp above the table cast a soft-focus glow over the two of them, leaving Jill and Garrett in drab shadow.

"Won't you join us?" asked Jill, pushing away the feeling of being a supporting character at her own meeting. "We were just finishing up business."

"Kindly excuse me," said Mr. Singh. "The snow calls me, and I must obey."

Jill looked outside at the snow falling thickly. "It's terrible weather, Mr. Singh. Maybe you should wait ..."

"All my life I've dreamed of winter," Amita said on cue. "So far I haven't caught a single snowflake on my tongue."

"Allow me the pleasure of making your dreams come

true," said Mr. Singh, extending his hand. And fantastically, Amita rose and, draping her coat over her shoulders, accepted it. Jill and Garrett sat open-mouthed as the two moved with musical grace out the door into the sudden blinding brilliance of sunlit snowflakes.

"He's a fast mover," said Garrett.

"That's the first time I've seen the sun this month," Jill marveled. The glow outside made the restaurant fade into dingy obscurity. Tinny Christmas tunes piped dolefully as she felt the weight of the Inn forcing her down into the ground. If only she could catch a warm salt breeze on her cheek. If only she could contemplate the vast expanse of the ocean.

"If only it would stop snowing," she whispered.

"What?" Garrett said.

"If only it would stop snowing," she said, louder. "No wonder the Inn is failing. Why would anyone come to a place with such an abysmal climate? Why would anyone even live in Ohio?"

"Not everyone can just walk away," said Garrett, not rising to her bait. "Some of us have jobs and family here."

The old fury was flaring up in Jill's chest. "For some of us, family is a job. Working with Mother doesn't just mean managing the Inn, it means managing her. I come out to do finances, I'm expected to declare my blind allegiance to whatever Mother wants. Everything I do is related to the family business. Nothing is simple. Nothing is straightforward."

Garrett was staring at her as if she'd begun to drool. "Jill, sometimes a job is just a job. Set the family business angle aside."

"What about you?" Jill demanded, suddenly angry at

him because he was kind. "Where's your independence? Where's your objectivity? What did you do to earn being where you are now? I thought you couldn't stand your family, but here you are getting rich off investing your dad's money."

"It's my money now, and well it should be," said Garrett sharply. "What's the matter with you? So you're angry with your mother. It gives you no right to be gratuitously rude and throw my family in my face when you don't have any idea what you're talking about anyway. Is this your *modus operandi*? When you're unhappy you lash out at the person closest to you? It's unattractive."

"What the hell is *modus operandi*?" Jill shouted. "Why should I care if you don't find me attractive? So what if I'm unattractive. I don't need a man to validate my appearance."

"I didn't say I don't find you attractive," said Garrett. "But your tactics right now are repulsive. Repulsive: that means the opposite of attractive; ergo, unattractive. *Modus operandi* means the way you work. I'm learning more than I'd like about that, at this moment."

He stood up and put on his hat. "Call me when you're in a better mood."

As he walked away from her, Jill wondered whether she should wait to break down until she was in her room, or complete her public disgrace and bawl right here in the restaurant. When Mother was cool in the face of a rage, it always seemed like she fully intended to be provoking. In Garrett's case, Jill sensed his disappointment, not just in her words, but in Jill herself. What, he'd hoped for something deeper? Maybe he'd thought she was a professional, or some emotionally competent person? Well, what if this was all there was to her—rage and reaction? Let him leave. See if she cared.

She cared.

She stood up to go after him, only to find herself confronted by a snow-blown Reagan.

"Do you even answer your phone anymore? I had to walk all the way over here to find you, and now my hair is ruined." She shook her lank locks accusingly at Jill.

"Wear a hat," Jill said, in no mood to be sympathetic to the failure of Reagan's blowout at the expense of losing Garrett.

"Look, you've got to help me," Reagan pleaded, pushing Jill back toward the table she'd come from. "Mother is out of control. Did you know she's been staying at my house? She's rearranged my pantry, fired my house cleaner that I've had for three years, and opened my mail. I told her she needs to go home, but she cries about being near her loved ones. If you were staying at the house, she wouldn't need to suffocate me."

"I'm not one of her 'loved ones,'" Jill retorted.

"Oh my God, Jill, you can't pay attention to anything Mother says. She gets that way. She'd probably welcome you with open arms if you would just talk to her. It's only fair to me."

"If I would just *talk* to her?" Could Reagan even hear herself? Did she realize how entitled, how disgustingly pampered she sounded? "I should be Mother's punching bag so you can have a night off?"

"Yes, exactly," Reagan agreed with relief. "I mean, tomorrow night she's taking Quennedey to midnight Mass, so I'll get a little quiet time then, but otherwise ..." She appealed to Jill with a gesture that was probably supposed to convey a weary candor. "I just can't take any more of her, Jill. I'm emotionally tapped out. Let's work together, get her back home in time for Christmas. It's what Daddy would have wanted."

Jill's small patience for this conversation ran out. "You should go home before it gets worse out there," she said, rising from the table.

"Think about what I've said." Reagan zipped her coat with purpose. "It's a time of love and joy, not a time to hold grudges. Show a little Christmas spirit."

Jill showed her to the door. "See you later."

Reagan paused in the doorway, for the first time seeming genuinely unsure of her words. "By the way, when I was coming in ... I mean ... does Mr. Singh dance?"

"Does he what?"

"Never mind," said Reagan hastily. "Only I thought I saw ... It must have been a trick of the light."

Overwhelmed by family, friends, and finance, Jill retreated to her room, where she collapsed face down on her bed and pondered whether even the Christmas spirit could paper over her mess of a life.

CHAPTER 10

EVER SINCE DECEMBER STARTED, THE OLD-TIMERS IN Luxembourg had been creaking in their rockers and predicting the worst winter since '78. But by Christmas Eve, even people tough enough to have walked to school uphill both ways were hard-pressed to sit on the porch and swap tales. The town was under a Level 3 snow emergency.

Jill spent the day at the Inn, since she couldn't go anywhere else. She checked the inventory of supplies. She consulted the service records for crucial systems: electrical, HVAC, backup generator. She reviewed employee scheduling and talked with the manager about skeleton staff and overtime pay. She did paperwork and accounts.

Amita helped with this, after a fashion, but she was floating in another genre, snowbound in a country inn with a tall, dark, handsome stranger. So was Jill, for that matter, but somehow Amita's holiday fantasy played out with lights and music, whereas Jill was stuck in a windowless office doing her mother's job. Would Amita still be having the time of her life if her parents were here with her? Jill had met Mr. and Mrs. Patel. They were peaceful and affectionate, a bit overbearing perhaps, but their daughter was clearly the joy of their lives. The Patels were a happy, loving family.

Did people call her own family a happy family? Did friends envy Mother her three established daughters? What did the O'Learys look like from the outside? Biblical, perhaps: Mother, the matriarch; Reagan, the mother; Del, the wife; and Jill, the prodigal daughter and now the resentful Older Brother as well, dutifully cleaning up messes without the promise of a fatted calf in the future. "Everything I have is yours," Mother had said, like the Father in the parable, but unlike the Father, she had not meant it as a statement of unconditional love.

Jill pushed aside her laptop. Time to stop grinding her teeth, and get some goodwill. So they were snowed in on Christmas Eve. Well, the Inn wasn't the worst place in the world to be. They had heat, they had a tree, and most importantly, they had food. And they were going to be jolly if it killed her. She stopped into the manager's office and announced that the Luxembourg Inn would host a hot chocolate social tonight for all snowbound guests.

THAT EVENING IN THE LOBBY, people chatted and laughed around the gas fireplace, holding festive paper cups of powdered cocoa sludge and plates of cheese and donut holes appropriated from the continental breakfast supply. A few intrepid souls were even trying to carol around the grand piano with the help of an iPad. Amita and Mr. Singh, basking in the flattering holiday glow of the Yule log, appeared to be ready for their close-up.

Jill, sipping her own cocoa, found the tension melting from her shoulders. She'd done it. She'd improved a bad situation. She'd made people happy. Food, fun, new friends —this was the essence of season's greetings, wasn't it? She had found her Christmas spirit.

A moment later she lost her Christmas spirit, when Reagan's name popped up on her phone.

"Jill, I need you to do me a favor." Reagan's voice was as tight as Saran Wrap over a bowl of Jell-O salad. "Go over to Mother's house and look through her medicine cabinet."

"What on earth? Why?"

"Because Mother took Quennedey to midnight Mass ..."

"But it's only 9:00."

"Midnight Mass can be whenever. It's just a phrase." Reagan dismissed Mass times as irrelevant. "Anyway, they left, and Mother forgot her phone here, and she got a text just now. It was an automated message from her pharmacy, reminding her that she hasn't refilled her prescriptions for a month."

"Wait," said Jill. "I thought you were joking when you said Mother had gone off her meds."

"I *was* joking!" Reagan sobbed. "Please, Jill, please. I need to know if Mother is driving my daughter in a blizzard when she hasn't taken her antidepressants in weeks."

"Why on earth did you agree to let Mother take her to church in this weather?" Jill demanded, following the first rule of crisis management: find someone to blame.

Reagan, for once, was open to self-recrimination. "I don't know. It's Christmas, and church, and Mother seemed so set on it, and Quennedey can be really exhausting, and it's nice to have someone else in charge of her for a while ..."

"I'm sorry," said Jill, more shaken by this new honesty of Reagan's than by anything else. "What do you want me to do?"

"Go over to Mother's and check her medicine bottles."

"How can I get in?"

"She always keeps a house key in her desk drawer there at the Inn. Go. Please. You can get there faster than I can in the snow."

"Okay, okay," said Jill, infected by Reagan's alarm. "I'm going now. Don't worry, Reagan. It's probably nothing."

Ten minutes later, bundled up in boots and coat and Daddy's sweater over her black dress, she dripped melted snow in Mother's bathroom as she stood with two bottles in her hand, doing hasty calculations as to date of prescription and dosage. The math was not reassuring. If Mother had been taking her medicine as prescribed, she would have run out at the beginning of December.

"Jill," Reagan wailed thinly over the phone. "Oh my god oh my god oh my god. I'm going out to get my baby."

"Reagan, listen to me," Jill pleaded. "Call Del to come over and sit with you. She lives so close it can't hurt if she drives a little bit. Let me go down to church and find Quennedey and bring her and Mother home. Reagan, do you hear me? Text me when Del gets there."

In the hallway, Jill tried to marshal her thoughts. Should she call the police? She pictured Mother's reaction to officers pushing their way through crowds of worshipers at St. Boniface, and quickly dismissed that idea. Quennedey probably wasn't in imminent danger. Mother had been living with Reagan for the past week without harming anything but Reagan's nerves. But the snow was apocalyptic. Mother shouldn't be driving in it with impaired judgment. Would Jill face penalties for going out during a snow emergency? But this also was an emergency, of a sort. Jill wished she had someone to call for advice and support.

Above her head, the white berries of the mistletoe gleamed in the light of the electric candles in the window. Jill felt a stab of longing. She sighed, swallowed her pride, and dialed Garrett.

"Garrett, please, I have a situation." She sounded pathetic, just like Reagan when she'd first called. "Mother took Quennedey to midnight Mass at St. Boniface ..."

"There is no midnight Mass," said Garrett.

"Yes, I know, it's at 10:00 or something. It's just a phrase."

"No, Jill, there's no midnight Mass at all. Level 3 snow emergency, everything was canceled. There will be Mass at St. Boniface tomorrow morning at 9:30. She said she was going to St. Boniface?"

"No," said Jill, her cold hands barely able to hold the phone. "She just said she was going to midnight Mass."

"The only parish anywhere around here holding a midnight Mass is Holy Infant in Milton Corner."

"Oh my God. That's in the next county, fifteen miles down a country road, at night." The room buzzed and swam for a moment. A chair rose up to support her. Grasping for anything to say that wasn't going to end up in Reagan-esque waterworks, she blurted, "How do you know all these schedules?"

"I'd been considering going to Holy Infant myself."

This bizarre statement functioned like a slap to jolt Jill out of her rising hysteria. "You're Catholic?"

"I'm in RCIA."

"Well, I never." That was the kind of dumb thing Daddy used to say in moments of shock. Great, she was turning into her father in her old age.

"Is there something strange about that?" Garrett asked.

"No! No, I mean ... I just thought being Catholic was something you left, not something you joined."

"How could there be an RCIA class if there weren't people wanting to join the Church?" Garrett said reasonably. Jill had no answer for that.

"So, your mom is taking Quennedey to Milton Corner," he said, back to business. "That's bad, but she'll call if they have a problem, right? Can you get hold of her?"

"She left her phone at Reagan's."

"Does Quennedey have a phone?"

"Yes, but she might not know there's a problem."

"How do you mean?"

"We just discovered that Mother probably hasn't taken her antidepressants for more than three weeks."

"Oh," said Garrett. "That explains a lot."

Jill was about to retort, but memories of Mother's recent behavior convinced her that Garrett, if anyone, had a right to make remarks.

"Reagan is freaking out," she said. "She wants Quennedey home now."

"Is Regina a threat?"

"I don't think so," said Jill uncertainly. "But taking a child on the back roads to Milton Corner in a Level 3 snow emergency is just about certifiable."

"The best thing to do would be to trace their route. It's mostly straight going. But on a night like this you'd need a snowplow to be sure of getting through safely."

"I do have a snowplow," Jill said, a light slowly dawning upon her. "Or at least, there's one at the garage. I'll call Heath Albany. He ought to drive out for us—I mean, technically, Mother owns the plow." She was suddenly urgent to be moving, doing anything to resolve this situation. "Thanks so much, Garrett. I'll call you back when I know something."

"But I'm ..." said Garrett, but Jill was already ringing off.

THERE WAS no point in calling the garage on Christmas Eve. As Heath's cell phone rang, Jill prayed that he was home, observing the snow emergency. Would God be mad if Heath's phone rang in church? Did Vineyard Fellowship even hold midnight services, or was that a Catholic thing? Surely a snowplow operator would know better than to go to church in this weather. Would Heath's wife be mad at Jill for asking him to drive out on Christmas Eve when he should be spending family time, or filling stockings, or assembling toys, or doing whatever parents did?

As usual, Jill was worried about all the wrong things.

"I'm completely blind," said Heath.

"Look," said Jill, fighting against the urge to fly off the handle again. "I know we have history, but I thought we were past that. If you don't want to go out because it's Christmas Eve, because it's me, just say so ..."

"I do want to help, don't get me wrong," protested Heath, who seemed aware of how feeble this excuse sounded, "but there is no way I can drive tonight. I literally cannot see. I've been in bed all day with snow blindness. It was the strangest thing. I was plowing the roads yesterday afternoon when the clouds broke, and the sun poured down like it was a summer day. It was blinding, like rainbows flashing everywhere. I had to call Angie to pick me up. I can barely open my eyes right now."

"Oh my God." In one way or another, people had been appealing to the Almighty all night. Was he ever going to answer? Maybe he was waiting for someone to show a little reverence. Jill drew a deep breath and breathed out a prayer. *God, send me a miracle.*

"I'm really sorry I can't help, but if you'd feel comfortable taking the snowplow out yourself..." Heath offered, stepping gingerly around her temper. "It's probably the safest thing you can drive tonight."

Thanks, God.

"I can't go alone," Jill protested, more to God than to Heath. "It's dangerous out there, I don't know what I'm looking for, it's been twelve years since I've driven to Milton Corner, and it's a pitch-black whiteout."

As if on cue, the doorbell rang. Garrett French, ridiculous in snow gear, wrapped up to his eyes, heaven-sent, stood on the porch.

"I started driving over as soon as you called," he said.

THE SNOWPLOW WAS heavy and warm, a moving fortress rumbling over the caked roads. Jill, at the wheel for insurance purposes, fought against the lure of false security as snowflakes drove hypnotically at her against the blackness.

These are the voyages of the snow ship Enterprise, floating on its five-year mission, in no way likely to skid off the road or get trapped in a drift.

"If this were a movie, we'd know exactly what we were trying to do," she complained to Garrett, as the truck crept past the last lights of town. "There would be some definite way to save the day. Maybe we'd rescue Mother and Quennedey from an accident, or take someone to the hospital, or deliver presents on Santa's behalf, or do something heroic. Instead, we're in a big-ass snowplow in a Level 3 snow emergency. On spec! A couple of chumps trying to get themselves killed."

"We'll be making sure Regina and Quennedey don't get themselves killed," Garrett pointed out. "There's nothing spec about that."

"Why are you being such a knight in shining armor about all this?" Jill demanded. "You don't have a personal stake in this fiasco. I'm snapping, I'm falling apart, I'm rude, and you don't even lose your temper."

"We can't both be losing our temper at the same time," Garrett replied, practical as always. He added, with only the slightest of preliminary deep breaths, "And I do have a personal stake."

A wave of warmth that had nothing to do with the blasting heater swept across Jill's cheeks. She swallowed hard and plunged in before he said anything else.

"Look, I need to apologize for my behavior yesterday. I don't know why I was so ugly to you. I'm an adult. I know I shouldn't take out my frustrations on people around me. And I do know—believe me, I do!—how destructive it is to hurl accusations at people just to get a rise. The only thing I know about your dad is that Mother thinks he's a good bludgeon to use against you. I am very sorry. And I've been sorry from the instant you walked away from the table."

She spared a glance away from the road to see if he had any reaction, but he was staring straight ahead in the faint green glow of the dashboard lights. As the silence stretched on, Jill's hopes began to deflate. When he'd said "personal stake," she'd taken that to mean that he was interested in her. What else could it mean? But probably he'd meant something emotionally repressed, and she'd jumped in and made a fool of herself. Again. So be it. An apology was never wasted. Perhaps this lesson in humility would finally teach her to stop and consider before opening her big mouth ...

"My parents got divorced when I was a few months old." Garrett, having marshaled his thoughts, interrupted Jill's internal monologue. "She was Black. He wasn't. I lived with Mom. She did her best, but even with the child support, it's not easy for a single mother with a high school diploma to make ends meet. We were always moving apartments. Mom bounced from one relationship to another. Some men treated her well. Others didn't. Meanwhile, my dad got remarried right away, to the blonde he was having an affair with. My brother is barely a year younger than I am. My dad's other family lived securely. When I went to his house on his weekends, I was a second-class citizen. His new wife didn't want me around —still doesn't, after thirty-five years. And my dad went along with it. Her house, her rules. His second marriage got all the hard work and sacrifice that he never gave to his first. And who cared?"

Now he was looking at her, and she was the one staring

straight ahead, rigid with the intensity of her listening. "Not the people at the church where my dad found Jesus. They saw a good husband to his wife, a good father to her son, saddled with this Black kid from his sinful past. They said everyone was welcome, but I wasn't welcome."

He started to light a cigarette, then caught himself. "Sorry, it's a tension thing. Replacing one addiction with another."

Jill let out the breath she'd been holding and dared to ask, "When did you start drinking?"

He shrugged. "In high school. All through college. After Mom died. I hit rock bottom—and your silver maple tree—ten years ago. Almost exactly. December 21." He laughed briefly, another tension thing. "Ten years, but people still remember. And maybe they're right. I caused a lot of harm. I don't want to gloss over that. But it's funny what you can be forgiven for. My dad earned forgiveness for abandoning my mom because he had a successful second marriage. But I didn't stop existing once he repented." He fidgeted with the unsmoked cigarette. "To be honest, I can barely look at my brother sometimes. It's not his fault. He's a good enough guy. I don't want to blame him for existing. I know how that feels. But I see his basic, normal life, every step right on time—college, job, house, nice wife, cute kids—and I wonder if that could have been me. Maybe I could have been a success too, if I'd had his advantages."

Garrett looked down at the crushed cigarette in his hand. *He doesn't know how good he is,* Jill thought, with a surge of hot compassion. *He doesn't know how glad I am he exists.*

"I don't know what you see in me," she said fiercely.

"From the inside, I look like a hot mess. But I can see you from the outside, and what I see looks pretty good. You're gracious and reliable and strong, and on top of that you look good in a hat. You have a little real-estate empire. You're sober ten years. You don't let my mother provoke you. I don't know if you realize how amazing that is to me. You already are a success."

"'If I have not love, I am nothing,' saith the apostle," quoth Garrett, with mild bitterness. "I'm also thirty-five, unmarried, childless, alone."

"I'm not a Scripture scholar," said Jill, wading determinedly into theological waters, "but I don't think the apostle was talking about the American Dream."

Garrett burst out laughing.

"Point to you," he said, "or to the apostle."

"While we're discussing all the awkward things," said Jill, wresting the conversation back from the apostle, "what is it about your dad's money? Why should my mother go on about it?"

"Because she likes to go on about things," he said. "There's nothing underhanded about it. My dad developed a conscience before he passed away and felt like he owed me something, which he did. So he left the bulk of his investments and his local property to me, rather than to my brother. His wife didn't forgive me for that, either, and we went a few rounds in court. I buy old buildings with architectural significance, and I restore them and rent them out. And downtown Luxembourg survives for one more generation, which your mom resents because it's not done on her terms."

He shrugged. Jill, having dashed waves of pity against the wall of his cool detachment, receded in exhaustion.

She'd been trying for days to spark some reaction in him: anger, joy, passion, any sign of life beneath his stoic facade. But he was too deep for her, and she was tired. If she couldn't match Garrett's reserve, she could at least stay safely on the level of easy cynicism.

"Mother ought to congratulate you," she said. "At least you've managed to give Luxembourg the patina of wholesome small-town charm. Fix up a few more crumbling buildings and the place will be irresistible to location scouts."

"Location scouts? Small-town charm?" Garrett was staring at her. "Do you think that's why I want to preserve downtown Luxembourg?"

"I don't know," said Jill. "I can't tell what you want."

"I don't give a rat's ass for location scouts, if that's what you think," said Garrett with startling sharpness. "I don't want Luxembourg to be picturesque so I can sell it to Hollywood. There's not much wholesome charm here these days. Do you know our county has a higher rate of overdose deaths than Cincinnati or Columbus?" The spark Jill had despaired of finally caught and flared up into a healthy blaze. "Do you know that our population has plummeted over the past decades? Do you know our unemployment stats? We are a community without hope. But even people in underpopulated, drug-addled Appalachia deserve to be proud of their architectural heritage. They deserve to have their history celebrated, not demolished to build another cheap soulless strip mall that will decay inside a decade. That's what I want. To give even people the rest of the country or the world considers trash the gift of their own history, preserved in the language of brick and stone. It matters because they matter. Every person in Luxembourg, every person in this county, every person on God's earth is worthy of beauty."

His countenance burned with the stern conviction of a prophet. Jill's scorched heart throbbed. She was almost panting. Were it not for the restraint of her seat belt, and the necessity of staying alive while operating a motor vehicle, she would have thrown herself into Garrett's arms. She opened her mouth to say, "I love you," but what came out, weakly, was, "Is it just me, or is it boiling in here?"

Garrett turned down the heat. "Look," he said, as evenly as if he had not just shattered the last wall between them. "There are the lights of Holy Infant. *Vincero.*"

THROUGH SOME DISCREPANCY in county protocols, Milton Corner was only at a Level 2 snow emergency. Holy Infant, on the outskirts of town, was on the cleared main road, and a number of brave souls had trusted to God and the road crews and come out for midnight Mass (at 10:00 p.m.). Mother's car occupied what was probably a coveted spot right next to the doors. Having parked the snowplow in the largest space she could find, Jill took off the ratty Christmas sweater and smoothed her black dress. She sent a reassuring text to Reagan and Del before she and Garrett crunched across the parking lot and slipped into a rear pew.

Mass was almost over. Everyone knelt after Communion as the choir warbled a hymn. In the front pew, sleek and pious, Mother bowed her head and Quennedey slumped beside her, half-asleep. Jill knelt beside Garrett and put her face in her hands. Relief and anxiety and anger and love and desire roiled inside her. So much for her peaceful Christmas spirit this evening. Here she'd done one brave thing and had one frank conversation and accomplished one mission, but it still wasn't enough. How could she break through Mother's facade and make her understand how much consternation she'd caused? Jill's slapping hand started to itch at the sight of Mother's perfect posture. Lord, where is my Christmas spirit? Make her understand. Make her hurt like I'm hurting.

She made herself look away from Mother toward the stable scene, with the chaos of shepherds and lambs and donkeys and oxen, and Joseph bending over to shield the mother and child, and in the midst of all the commotion Mary contemplating only her baby Jesus, pinkly serene in his swaddling clothes.

This is not your fight, the mother said to her.

Not literally. The mouth of the statue didn't move, and the expression didn't change. But Jill heard the words in a mother's voice—not her own mother's voice, and not her own voice, which had never said anything maternal ever. She resisted. Why should it not be my fight? I want it to be my fight. I'm hurting. I'm a casualty. Why should I not strike a blow for justice and responsibility?

This is not your fight.

Hmph, Jill thought. Whose fight is it, then?

Let the baby handle it.

Oh my God, groaned Jill for the umpteenth time that evening. What does a baby know about handling anything? She regarded the plaster infant, more oblivious than any living child. Indeed, there were living children in the congregation. A few pews in front of her, a real baby fussed and writhed as its mother jogged him on her lap. You go, kid, thought Jill. You handle it.

"Veil'd in Flesh, the Godhead see," the choir intoned in ponderous harmony. Jill contemplated the baby in front of her as if he were the baby Jesus. See baby Jesus suddenly buck and bang his Godhead on the pew in front of him. See his frustrated mother scoop him up and rush him down the aisle. See the Godhead, Veil'd in Flesh, bawling, big tears rolling down his screwed-up face.

Poor little kid, Jill thought, as the screaming infant was swept past her. At least baby Jesus knows what you're going through.

Mother seemed completely unfazed to see them after Mass.

"So, you came to church after all," she said to Jill. "You might have told me beforehand. We all could have driven out together."

"We're all going to drive back together," said Jill lightly, borrowing a little Silent Night from baby Jesus sleeping in his stable. "We'll come back later in the week and get your car."

THE DRIVE HOME WAS ANTICLIMACTIC. Garrett kept up a running light chatter with Mother and deflected any explosive subjects. Oblivious to any snow emergency, Quennedey snuggled up against Jill's arm and slept. Jill, whose main desire was to get home alive and awake, was now disinclined to pick a fight. She was at that state of weariness in which her consciousness seemed to float above her body. Her hands moved the wheel on autopilot, steering the plow gently through the streaky whiteness that extended forever past the headlights. In a daze, she escorted Mother and Quennedey to the front door, where

Reagan stood waiting with her arms crossed, tear-stained, tight-lipped. This is not your fight, she thought as she pulled away again. This is not your fight.

Still on autopilot, Jill turned in to the Inn gates and sat, heavy-lidded, as the lights of the parked plow illuminated the snowflakes against Mother's house. Beside her, Garrett stirred drowsily.

"Am I going home?" he mumbled. "My car is at the garage."

"You can sleep in my bed," said Jill.

"Ah?" said Garrett, opening his eyes. "And where will you be?"

"In Mother's bed."

Garrett held the Dad sweater as Jill fished stupidly in her purse for the key. In the hallway, they halted under the mistletoe, more from obligation than anything else. Jill rested her weary forehead against Garrett's, unsure whether the first faint stirring of felicity meant she was waking up or finally falling asleep.

"Merry Christmas," murmured Garrett.

"Merry Christmas," Jill whispered.

As if on cue, they both yawned fit to split their heads open. With mutual wordless consent, they dragged themselves upstairs and shut their respective doors.

CHAPTER 11

THE DOOR OPENED, AND A VOICE SAID, "JILL, GET OUT of Mother's bed."

Jill grunted and tucked the blankets under her chin. A moment later they were pulled back, and the lamp beside the bed glared painfully in her face.

"Get up," said Del. "Mother needs to lie down."

Jill sat up, blinking. Del was standing beside the bed with her arm around Mother. Mother radiated the remains of a tragic dignity. Smudges of mascara had been inexpertly wiped from her face. Her hair, so precise at midnight Mass, looked now like it had been styled with a cattle prod. Bleary as she was, Jill felt a jolt of alertness.

"Is something wrong?" she asked.

"Everything's fine," said Del, in a voice that said that everything was certainly not fine. "Mother just needs to go to bed, so you get up."

"No, no," Mother murmured. "Jill shouldn't have to move when she's been working so hard all night long. I'll go sleep in her bed."

"You can't!" yelped Jill, bolting up and standing in the doorway in what she hoped was a casual attitude.

"Why not?"

"Because Garrett French is in my bed."

It was not easy to catch Del off her stride, but this tidbit took her a moment to process. Mother, rallying her signature spirit, remarked, "And you're in mine. No wonder you're still single, Jill."

"Go to bed, Mother," Del commanded softly, and to Jill's astonishment, Mother climbed right into bed, hair, makeup, clothes, and all. Del steered Jill out of the room and shut the door.

In the hallway, a cold gray light came through the windows over the stairs. "What time is it?" Jill whispered.

"Seven in the morning."

"Why are you guys up so early?" moaned Jill. "It's Christmas."

"We haven't been to bed yet," said Del shortly. "If you're making coffee, make me some."

She disappeared into the bathroom. Jill glanced longingly at her own bedroom door, where the Dad sweater was slumbering with Garrett, then took herself downstairs. She stumbled around the cold kitchen in last night's little black dress, wrapped in a Christmas afghan she snatched from the back of a couch. Pickings were slim, as Mother had been at Reagan's for more than a week, but there were pods for the Keurig machine. If the coffee would not be lovingly hand-crafted, at least it would be fast.

Feet shuffled down the stairs. Jill turned around and gasped to see Daddy, angles and proportions and colors all absurd, enter the kitchen. An instant later, the image resolved into Garrett, entirely correct, wearing the Christmas sweater over the jeans he'd slept in. Either way, Jill wanted to throw herself into his arms and feel Daddy's sweater wrapped around her.

The sweater she would get, at least. Startled by her initial shock, Garrett was all apologies. "I wanted something warm. I hoped it wouldn't bother you if I wore the Dad sweater," he said, pulling it off. Jill had a glimpse of abs as his T-shirt slid up.

"You didn't have to," she protested, without force, as he handed her the sweater.

"We'll trade," he said. "Gimme the blanket."

Del walked in as Jill was wriggling her way into the sweater and Garrett was draping himself like a chieftain. She went straight to Jill's mug of coffee and downed it black.

"Long night?" Jill asked.

Del sat at the table. "Reagan called the paramedics on Mother because she threatened to kill herself," she said.

Jill and Garrett both stared open-mouthed. "What happened?" Jill asked.

"Nothing that needed to happen," said Del. "Reagan was angry and wanted to stage a big intervention. I told her she should wait until Mother was on her meds again. But she had to make a big scene and demand an accounting from Mother right then, and of course Mother got defensive and angry. She and Reagan screamed at each other for a long time and raked up every grievance on the books."

"I'm glad I wasn't there," said Jill, awed.

"Me too," said Del. "You would only have made it

worse. Finally, Mother got dramatic and said she would be better off dead."

"Did she try to hurt herself?" asked Garrett.

"Of course not," said Del. "Mother loves herself too much for that. But it was a stupid thing to say, and Reagan jumped on it and called 911. Reagan and Mother both sobered up when the paramedics came, and they had to deal with the assessment and the paperwork. I talked with one of them about whether Mother needed to go to the ER and get her prescriptions filled right away, but we agreed that sitting in the ER for hours would only agitate her more and be a waste of money."

"She still has some pills here," said Jill. "Can't she start on those?"

"She says they make her feel sick, so we need to get an appointment and see if we can adjust the dosage or try something different," said Del. "I'm going to stay with her today and make sure she gets some rest, so you should probably leave."

"Fine," said Jill, feeling stung. Of course, she and Mother didn't get along, but she wasn't about to stir up Reagan levels of drama.

"You don't have to be pissy," said Del. "It just makes sense for today, until she regulates. One reason Mother stopped taking her meds was because you were coming back. She said she was embarrassed that the reason you were coming home after all these years was because she couldn't manage Daddy's finances. She felt like she'd failed him and the whole family by not being able to carry on by herself, without pills."

"That's really stupid," said Jill, almost nauseated with

humiliation and rage. "I will not take the blame for this. No part of this is my fault."

A warm mug of coffee was placed in her furious hands, and Garrett was tucking the afghan around her.

"No one's blaming you," said Del. "Mother is all messed up with grief and guilt. This morning she saw how toxic she looks from the outside. She thinks she can just say anything and there won't be any consequences. The paramedics don't take the same view."

Jill was resolutely absorbed by her mug, so Garrett asked, "What happens now?"

"Mother isn't good at living alone," said Del. "And she can't live with Reagan, and Jill can't live with her. Scott and I have been talking about moving to Albuquerque. Mother will come with me."

She sipped her coffee. Jill's head swam. She felt bludgeoned by the events of the morning. This last twist was too much to take in. She herself had moved to the other side of the country to get away from Mother, and here was Del proposing to move Mother in with her like it was that easy.

"Have you talked to Regina about this?" asked Garrett dubiously.

"Not yet, but Mother will usually listen to me," said Del. "She makes noise about going to Florida, but she was counting on Daddy to make the arrangements. So long as I do the work, she'll talk a good game about plans, and eventually she'll claim it was all her idea in the first place."

"Well, I never," said Jill.

Garrett focused on practicalities. "What about the businesses?"

Del shrugged off the businesses. "She's giving the hotel

to Jill, isn't she? And Reagan will get that useless piece of land. The garage will finally go to Heath Albany—Daddy should have sold it to him years ago."

Jill finally found her voice. "What's Mother going to live on? Is Scott going to make her an allowance? Who's going to finance her pills and counseling and shopping and trips?"

"Mother's old enough to be on Medicare. And you can sell the house and send her the money." Del stood up and stretched. "I'm going to sleep now. See you later."

Jill flung her arms around her warm, solid sister. "I love you, Cordelia," she mumbled into Del's coarse hair. "Merry Christmas."

"I love you too," said Del. "You should take a shower."

She stumped off to bed, leaving Jill and Garrett to their coffee and recalibration.

"What now?" Jill finally said.

"Well, we've got a snowplow," said Garrett. "Want to go to Christmas Mass at 9:30 at St. Boniface?"

"Dressed like this?" Jill surveyed her rumpled dress and Garrett's jeans and t-shirt.

"I think it's justifiable to say that God won't care."

They opened the front door and immediately recoiled from the glittering assault. Beyond the shadows of the porch, the new sunlight refracted into every color and resolved into crystalline fluff. The world had been freshly washed and bleached and hung out to melt.

"A Christmas miracle," said Garrett, taking Jill's arm. "It's stopped snowing."

CHAPTER 12

I N THE SLOW-NEWS PERIOD BETWEEN CHRISTMAS AND
New Year's Eve, word leaked out in Luxembourg County
that at a poorly attended meeting of the Green Township
trustees on December 24, the BlueStone Development
Group submitted an application to rezone 60 acres of
scrubland down by the highway, from agricultural use to
planned commercial development. Along with this application, BlueStone, represented by Amit Singh, also
submitted preliminary plans for an outlet mall to be built
on this same parcel. At once, speculation began. Bidding
wars erupted for plots that had been worthless a week
before. Local businesses began to make five-year plans for
improvements and renovations based on the proposed
crowds of bargain-hungry shoppers soon to descend. A few
crotchety landowners vowed to fight the rezoning tooth
and nail, but most of Luxembourg County was desperate
for economic revival. There was little doubt that within 24
months, the BlueStone Outlet would have a triumphant
ribbon-cutting ceremony.

Devoted outlet mall shoppers are a breed apart. They spend in multi-day sprees, and at the end of the day, they need somewhere to stay and store their treasures. And there was, at present, one established lodging in minute Luxembourg, Ohio: the Luxembourg Inn, proprietor-to-be Gillian O'Leary.

"I feel like I've just been pushed out of a plane, and I'm about to find out whether my parachute works," said Jill to Garrett, Mr. Singh, and Amita, all gathered around a table at the Inn's restaurant. "I'm miles up and I'm not dead yet, but I'm going to need a landing plan real soon."

"You won't have any trouble getting a loan application through now," Garrett said. "You're positioned to be the prestige option for shoppers and tourists who want local flavor. And you have at least two years to complete your upgrades and be ready. The chain hotels will be starting from the ground up. We'll need to look at the proposal to see what we're competing against."

Mr. Singh held up a hand. "BlueStone's proposal only covers retail. Hotels will need to be proposed and built separately by independent developers." He smiled seraphically. "I enjoy the Luxembourg Inn, myself."

"I haven't quite figured out how I'm going to balance everything," Jill said. "Hotel proprietor in Ohio, accountant in California. Amita, can you believe we'll be going back to Los Angeles after all this? No more snow, for a start."

"Actually," said Amita shyly, exchanging a private glance with Mr. Singh. "Amit and I are going to his family's compound in Hyannisport for a few days. I'm going to meet his mother."

Once again Jill's ears buzzed with the twang of a

distant sitar. First thing I fix is the sound system in here, she thought as everyone stood up. Amita seized her in a fierce hug and whispered, "Wish me luck! His mother is very old-fashioned."

"Every good thing," Jill wished her, with a squeeze for emphasis.

"Maybe we'll both be quitting soon," Amita murmured in her ear. Mr. Singh shook Garrett's hand and exchanged business cards. Then he took Jill's hand and held it briefly to his lips, as he had at the white elephant party.

"Farewell, Miss O'Leary," he said, as cool and thrilling as ever. "I look forward to a successful future partnership."

The twanging swelled and then receded as Mr. Singh and Amita exited, arm in arm. Jill rubbed her ear to rid it of the last droning note.

"How cagey that man is," Garrett said. "'A successful future partnership.' Partnership with whom? With you? With the Inn? With Amita? A generic future partnership? He promises everything, equivocally."

"With Reagan, maybe," Jill said. "It's probably thanks to him that she nabbed Dad's property by the highway."

"She ought to sell now," said Garrett. "By the time BlueStone is making offers, they'll be driving hard bargains. Right now, people are crazy. They'll pay anything for that land. Unless she really does want to build her forever home there."

Jill scoffed absently at the idea of Reagan's forever home. She had already dismissed Mr. Singh's parting words and was meditating on Amita's. Quit her job? She had never considered running the Inn as a viable option. The financials were a mess. But even if they had been entirely solid, how could anyone have full autonomy while Mother was still near enough to drop in to ensure that things were being run her way? Now, however, blessed Del was taking Mother on and moving her far across time zones and almost over the continental divide.

Visions of an alternate future danced in her head, one in which Mother was a mentor and guide to her as they worked through the Inn renovations together. In which she could draw fearlessly on Mother's intuitive design sense because Mother wouldn't take the rejection of her ideas personally. In which they had a partnership built on mutual respect and expertise.

In this fallen world, however, some people were better loved at a distance. For years, that distance had been the divide between Los Angeles and Luxembourg. Now there was no barrier to coming home: not Heath Albany's dog, not Mother herself, not even bad career prospects. Certainly, not close ties in Los Angeles. Her best friend there was ready to embark on her own adventure.

And some people were better loved up close, in person.

EARLY ON THE morning of New Year's Eve, Garrett was on the porch once more, knocking on Mother's door. Jill answered, wrapped in scarf and puffy coat.

"Well, I'm here," he said, wiping the mud from his feet. "And it was hard enough to get up to the house, between the melting snow and the trucks in your driveway. What's going on?"

Jill held out her hand. "Will you take a walk with me?"

They strolled down the driveway toward the street. It

had not snowed since Christmas Day, and in the more typical December weather the pristine snowscape had been slowly melting down into slush and muck and big dirty plowed mounds. The trucks had churned up what was left of the snow by the gates where the silver maple leaned. A man in a cherry picker wielded a chainsaw in the tree's top branches. Crews at the bottom trimmed the fallen sections into logs and loaded up the brush to be fed into a chipper.

"You're getting rid of the silver maple," Garrett stated, not needing to phrase it as a question since the answer was before his eyes.

"I don't want a monument to your past mistakes," Jill said. "It's time to plant something new and straight."

They watched, fingers living and entwined, as limb after limb fell from the great slanted trunk. When all branches were gone, and the men began to slice into the twenty-foot long main trunk, the man in the cherry picker gave a shout. He reached out and grasped the edge of the raccoon's hole, and easily rocked the huge column back and forth.

"Hollow!" he yelled. "All the way down."

As slices of the trunk tumbled down, the rotten core crumbled. Garrett walked away from Jill and stared down at a thin ring of wood, five feet in diameter.

"All this time I thought I'd ruined this tree," he said, his back to her. "Me, with my own stupid choices and addiction, I destroyed it single-handedly, and every time someone looked at it, they could say, 'Garrett French did that. It's all Garrett's fault.' Sometimes I thought I didn't die when I hit the tree only because God wanted me alive as an object lesson. And all the time, here is what was at the center of all my guilt and self-loathing. Nothing. Nothing at all."

He ground a piece of crumbly wood into powder under his heel and contemplated the nothingness of the dust with the shattered wonder most people reserved for the vastness of the Grand Canyon or the terror of an eclipse.

"I thought I wasn't safe," he said softly. "I thought I damaged everything I touched. And the silver maple was solid scientific evidence that I ruined things when I wasn't under control. Sometimes I wished that I'd died that night. It seemed a cruel fluke that I hadn't been killed."

"I'd hoped you'd be happy," Jill stammered, unnerved by the open emotion in his voice. "I didn't mean to upset you."

He turned to her. Instead of the tight, ravaged expression she'd come to expect from him in times of tension, something had unlocked inside him. His brown eyes were still fathomless wells, but the water at the bottom was newly sweet and clear and cold.

"I was wrong," he said, almost joyfully. "I had it all wrong. When I hit the tree, the hollow trunk must have absorbed the blow and cushioned most of the shock. I didn't destroy the silver maple. It saved my life."

"I'm glad," she said, working her chilled fingers back between his. "To be honest, I'd rather have you than the tree."

They walked hand in hand back to the house, splattering through the dirty, salty slush. Garrett was still rapt in contemplation of his own private miracle. Jill knew she should have been delighted for him, but his alien sense of peace was a new wall between them. He was healing before her eyes, becoming undamaged, all because of a stupid tree. He would become whole and stable, needing no comfort or support from anyone, especially not from someone as broken as Jill O'Leary.

As the front door shut on the chaos in the yard, Jill looked up. The ball of mistletoe dangled in the center of the hall, suspended only by a fine clear thread that glinted in the cold morning light.

"Piss off," she told it.

"What do you have against mistletoe?" Garrett asked, close and confident by her side. "I like it, myself."

"It mocks me," she snapped, lashing out against his new-found closure. "It seems so inviting, but it's still Mother's mistletoe, in Mother's hallway, in Mother's house. I can't let that go. I don't even know what's wrong with me. Maybe I've never really grown up. I'm nothing more than an edgy teenager, knocking over Mother's tree and flirting in her hall." She wrenched her hand from his with the ruthlessness of one ripping out tender young roots. "It's not fair to you. Let's go somewhere else."

"It's too muddy," Garrett said, not seeming to care what was fair to him. "Let's stay here and watch the tree come down. I'll make cocoa. I'm good at it."

"Are you even listening to me?" Jill knew she was on the verge of tears again, and it made her even angrier. "This is not my home. So long as I'm somewhere dominated by Mother, I can't change. I can't grow up enough to have a real relationship or start my own family. It sounds so pathetic when I say it out loud."

"I think it sounds human," said Garrett. "And I want a relationship with a human, a struggling, suffering, beautiful human. Who happens to own a hotel I've been thinking about buying. I love you."

Jill stared at him, standing in Mother's hall as fearless as if he owned the place.

"Are you expecting me to say 'I love you' back?" she demanded.

"I'd like that."

"I think you're serious," she said, aggressively tamping down any rebellious spark of hope, "because you usually are. But this time you're wrong if you're under the impression that love is suddenly going to give us a happy ending. I used to think I was a stable person. Now here I am, back in the middle of everything I tried to run away from, and I'm realizing that I was only running away from how messed up I truly am. Real happiness won't look like escape."

"But it might look like recovery," Garrett said. "One step forward and two steps back. We could at least walk together."

Jill shrugged defensively. "Sure, that would be nice. You can be my mentor or something." She yanked open the door, welcoming the cold draft and the blast of pandemonium. "I promised myself that I wouldn't kiss you in Mother's house," she shouted over the furious whine of the woodchipper. "Where to?"

"My house," Garrett said, setting his hat on the hall table.

Jill groaned with impatience. "Let's get started, then."

"Fine." He put his hand over hers on the knob and closed the door, pushing away her protective barrier of noise and chill. She wanted to fight with him, to make him as nervous and frustrated as she was, but all her objections were stilled by the quiet shock of his hands unwrapping her scarf, unzipping her coat, sliding it off her shoulders.

"Regina accepted my offer this morning." The warmth of his mouth set the life racing back through her numb forehead and nose and lips. "Ergo, you're in my house now."

Jill took a great shuddering breath. "Garrett, if you're joking, I will kill you. I mean it. I've run over a dog before."

"I want to hear all about it." He pulled her close. "But not right now."

After a delicious, frantic interlude that melted any slush left on the two of them, Jill pulled back and gasped, "I hope you lowballed her."

"Not at all," Garrett answered, between slower kisses. "I figured ... I was doing my part ... to set her up ... far away from here."

"Well, you're a fast mover," Jill murmured. "If I'm going to move back from Los Angeles, now I'm going to have to find myself a place to live."

"Here, I hope. Eventually."

Jill disentangled herself enough to get a good look at his face. "Are you ... proposing to me?"

Garrett didn't let her go. "Not just yet. We barely know each other. I think we both have a lot of healing to do before we're able to make vows. But I'm going to keep the mistletoe up until the day I carry you over the threshold."

"And I'll keep it up every day after that," Jill promised, relaxing into the mostly stable, entirely felicitous reality of right now, in snowy, forested, small-town Luxembourg, Ohio, where the population is, at this moment, 5,001.

❄

ABOUT THE AUTHOR

Cat Hodge lives in Delaware, OH, with her husband Brendan and their seven children. This is her first published novel. Her other novels are jealous.

To learn about future releases, subscribe to the Oak & Linden newsletter:

http://www.oakandlinden.com/p/newsletter_24.html

ACKNOWLEDGMENTS

My husband Brendan is my first reader, my best critic, and my unfailing support. His friendship and love brings joy to my life; his business savvy made this project possible, and fun. Likewise, my children—Eleanor, Julia, Isabel, Jack, Diana, William, and Paul—have never grudged me my writing time, or the haphazard household management that ensues.

Dr. Monica Anderson and Shawn Dougherty channeled my unfocused theatrical ambitions into a love of the dramatic structure at the foundation of all great stories.

Brandon Watson, polymath, found the perfect title for the story by knowing where to look for it.

Joanne McPortland, John Herreid, and Suzanne T. Fortin all provided invaluable technical and creative assistance.

Rosamund Hodge, Leah and Alexi Sargent, Sherwood Smith, Kirsten Kinnell, Amy Carney, and Brett and Flannery Salkeld patiently read drafts and hunted for errors.

No one could ask for more appreciative readers than Mom, Dad, and Mum—Amy Egan, Paul Egan, and Mary Hodge.